CW00530219

TO THE
BATMOBILE...!

CLASSIC TV

In 1966, Batman burst on to the nation's TV screens, and captured the free-wheeling mood of the times. Its dazzling sets and colorful costumes, celebrity guest stars and comedic, action-packed plots, appealed to viewers of all ages. Batmania had hit the mainstream!

With tongue-in-cheek characterization and fantastical storylines it was an instant hit, and it remains a classic. But nothing in the show matched the flamboyance of the incredible vehicles. Based on their fabulous comic-book predecessors, they looked spectacular on screen. They were customized from real cars, boats and bikes, and were specially created for Batman, Robin and their adversaries by teams of expert engineers and designers.

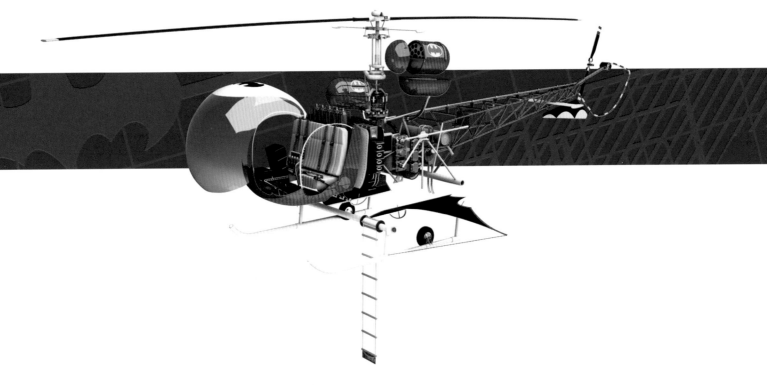

BATMOBILE CUTAWAYS

The cutaways featured in this magazine were specially commissioned by editor and comics expert Richard Jackson in conjunction with DC Comics. The annotated artwork enables you to peel back the layers and see not only under the bonnet but also inside the gadgets of these extraordinary machines. All the key vehicles from the 1966 Batman movie, the 1966-67 live-action TV series and the first animated TV series from 1968 are revealed in extraordinary detail.

With specifications and a special features listing, with words from Batmobile expert James Hill, this is the definitive guide to Live Action Batmobiles.

CONTENTS

THE WHEELED
WONDER

THE BATMAN TV SERIES OF 1966 WAS UNLIKE ANY OTHER SHOW. THE COLORFUL, POP-ART SETS, ALONG WITH THE CELEBRITY GUEST STARS AND THE OVER-THE-TOP PLOTS, ENSURED THAT ADULTS AND CHILDREN WERE GLUED TO THEIR SETS.

Featured in all 120 episodes, as well as the movie based on the series, the Batmobile of the 1966 TV series has become one of the most widely recognized cars of all time. At least once an episode, Batman and Robin would leap from the Batpole into the seats of the Batmobile and utter this famous phrase: (Robin) "Atomic batteries to power. Turbines to speed." (Batman) "Roger. Ready to move out." The Batmobile would then race out of the Batcave and the Dynamic Duo's adventure would truly begin. The Batman and Robin of the 1960s TV series were colorful, larger-than-life characters who showed true dedication to fighting crime. The Dynamic Duo were all-American heroes, and so the Batmobile needed to capture their style and charisma. With

its tail-fins, headlights, bubble dome and distinctive red trim, the Batmobile had a personality equal to that of the show's main stars. Used primarily to transport Batman and Robin around Gotham City, the Batmobile also contained a wealth of gadgets that allowed the Dynamic Duo to foil the crimes of their assorted enemies. In one episode the Batmobile might be used as a surveillance device, with Batman utilizing the onboard monitors to keep track of the Riddler or King Tut; in another episode the Batmobile would save the day by stopping an escaping villain with its headlight laser rays. The TV show Batmobile was a truly amazing vehicle, whose only limitations were the imaginations of Batman and, of course, the show's writers.

ORIGINS

THE BATMOBILE FROM THE '60S HAS BECOME ONE OF THE MOST ICONIC VEHICLES IN TELEVISION HISTORY. FOR THOSE INVOLVED IN ITS DESIGN THE CHALLENGE WAS TO TURN FORD'S CONCEPT CAR INTO A VEHICLE BEFITTING THE DYNAMIC DUO.

The Ford Lincoln Futura

Costing $250,000 to produce in a factory in Turin, Italy, the Futura was considered too expensive and, like many concept cars, abandoned after just one vehicle was produced. Picked up by George Barris of Barris Kustom City in the mid-1960s, reportedly for the measly sum of $1, the concept car found a new lease on life when in August 1965, the producers of the Batman TV series approached George and asked him to build a Batmobile. With filming set to begin in less than three weeks, the veteran car mechanic decided that the Futura already had enough 'Bat' like qualities to make it the ideal template. With a few modifications to the bodywork and the addition of gadgets the Batmobile was born.

CONCEPT DESIGNS

The Batmobile was designed from the ground up to be more than just an 'iconic fast car.' The large body not only made sure all conceivable gadgets could be concealed within, but also made it possible to house a large turbo-charged engine, complete with 'atomic batteries.' The twin fins on the Batmobile's outer shell gave the car a certain 'bat' quality as well as maximizing downforce to keep the car firmly on the road at high speeds.

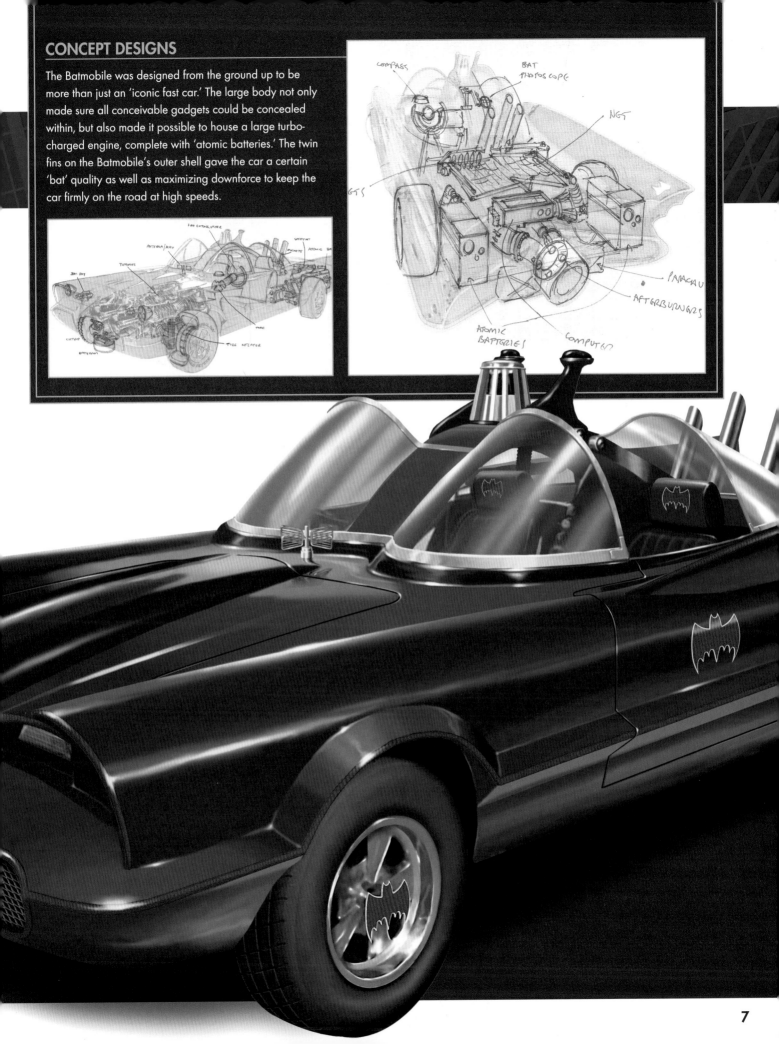

WHILE THE BATMOBILE'S ICONIC BODYWORK
AND STRIKING SYMBOLS WOULD COME TO HAUNT
THE DREAMS OF BATMAN'S GREATEST VILLAINS,
IT WAS THE VEHICLE'S GADGETS THAT WOULD
TIME AND AGAIN FOIL THEIR NEFARIOUS PLOTS.

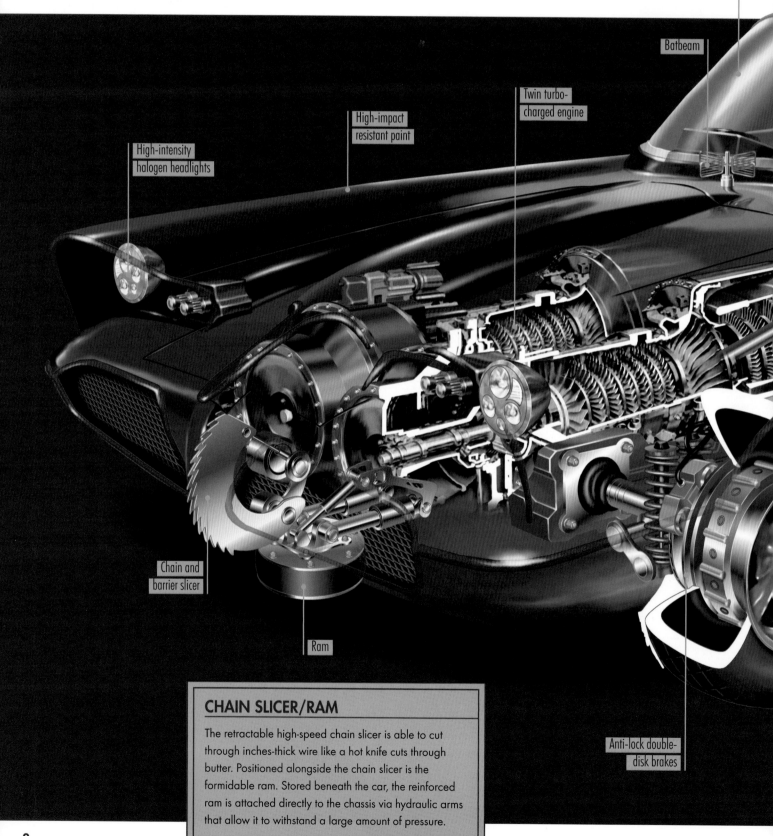

Bullet-proof, reinforced
transparent thermoplastic

Batbeam

Twin turbo-
charged engine

High-impact
resistant paint

High-intensity
halogen headlights

Chain and
barrier slicer

Ram

Anti-lock double-
disk brakes

CHAIN SLICER/RAM

The retractable high-speed chain slicer is able to cut
through inches-thick wire like a hot knife cuts through
butter. Positioned alongside the chain slicer is the
formidable ram. Stored beneath the car, the reinforced
ram is attached directly to the chassis via hydraulic arms
that allow it to withstand a large amount of pressure.

THE BATBEAM

Utilizing different frequencies in the electromagnetic spectrum, the Batbeam is capable of not only detecting and disarming all manner of explosives but can also cut through solid steel doors. When activated, the Batbeam antenna rises from the center of the bonnet and fires its rays at the designated target.

Police siren and rotating light

Emergency flashing strobe lights

Wheel-slashing hubcaps

Dual-coil suspension

High-pressure ejector seat

Automatically inflating tire

THE EJECTOR SEAT

Able to be triggered remotely, the ejector seat uses high-pressured air canisters to launch the seat and occupant more than 300 feet into the air. A parachute device attached to the back of the seat guides it safely to the ground. Primarily used to eject villains who had stolen the Batmobile, this system could also be used by Batman and Robin to save themselves from fatal collisions.

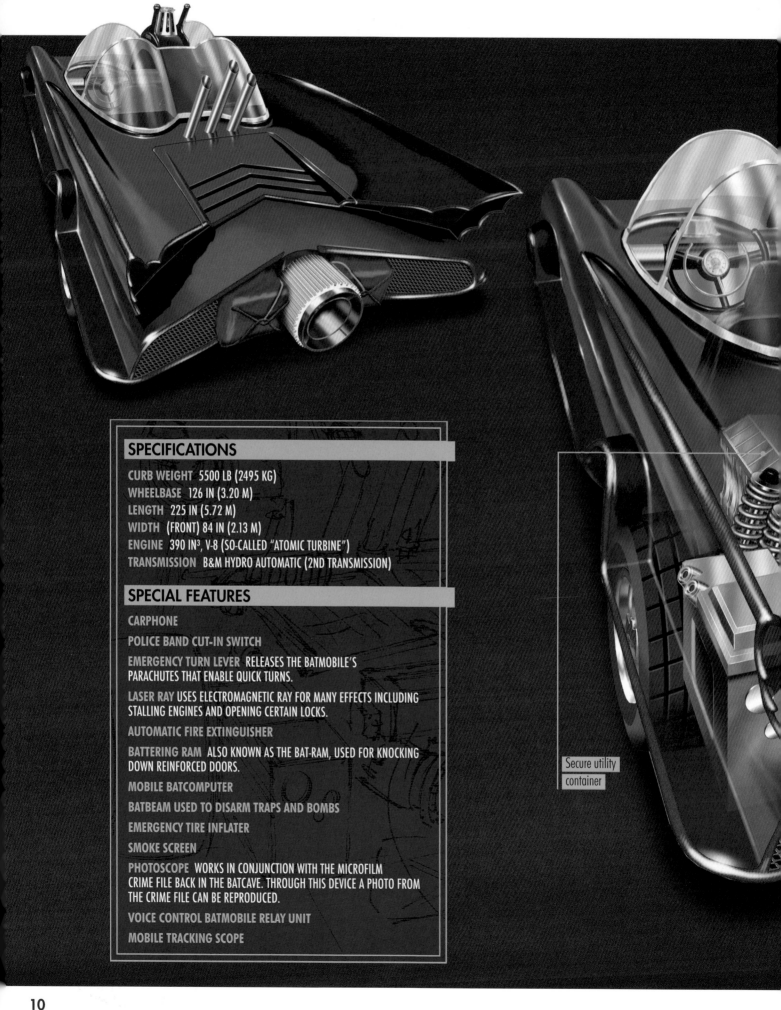

SPECIFICATIONS

CURB WEIGHT 5500 LB (2495 KG)
WHEELBASE 126 IN (3.20 M)
LENGTH 225 IN (5.72 M)
WIDTH (FRONT) 84 IN (2.13 M)
ENGINE 390 IN³, V-8 (SO-CALLED "ATOMIC TURBINE")
TRANSMISSION B&M HYDRO AUTOMATIC (2ND TRANSMISSION)

SPECIAL FEATURES

CARPHONE

POLICE BAND CUT-IN SWITCH

EMERGENCY TURN LEVER RELEASES THE BATMOBILE'S
PARACHUTES THAT ENABLE QUICK TURNS.

LASER RAY USES ELECTROMAGNETIC RAY FOR MANY EFFECTS INCLUDING
STALLING ENGINES AND OPENING CERTAIN LOCKS.

AUTOMATIC FIRE EXTINGUISHER

BATTERING RAM ALSO KNOWN AS THE BAT-RAM, USED FOR KNOCKING
DOWN REINFORCED DOORS.

MOBILE BATCOMPUTER

BATBEAM USED TO DISARM TRAPS AND BOMBS

EMERGENCY TIRE INFLATER

SMOKE SCREEN

PHOTOSCOPE WORKS IN CONJUNCTION WITH THE MICROFILM
CRIME FILE BACK IN THE BATCAVE. THROUGH THIS DEVICE A PHOTO FROM
THE CRIME FILE CAN BE REPRODUCED.

VOICE CONTROL BATMOBILE RELAY UNIT

MOBILE TRACKING SCOPE

Secure utility
container

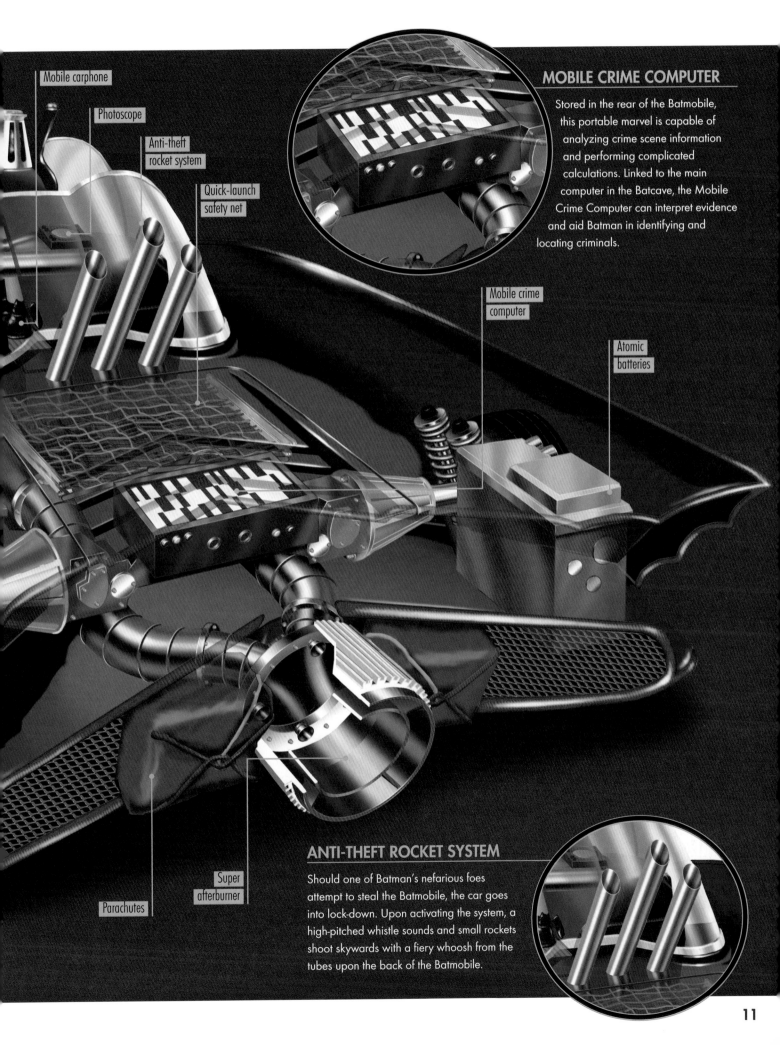

Mobile carphone

Photoscope

Anti-theft rocket system

Quick-launch safety net

MOBILE CRIME COMPUTER

Stored in the rear of the Batmobile, this portable marvel is capable of analyzing crime scene information and performing complicated calculations. Linked to the main computer in the Batcave, the Mobile Crime Computer can interpret evidence and aid Batman in identifying and locating criminals.

Mobile crime computer

Atomic batteries

Super afterburner

Parachutes

ANTI-THEFT ROCKET SYSTEM

Should one of Batman's nefarious foes attempt to steal the Batmobile, the car goes into lock-down. Upon activating the system, a high-pitched whistle sounds and small rockets shoot skywards with a fiery whoosh from the tubes upon the back of the Batmobile.

A DREAM MACHINE

WHEN THE PERFIDIOUS PENGUIN MADE OFF WITH THE BATMOBILE, BATMAN WHEELED OUT HIS FIRST BATCYCLE. WHILE NOT AS FLAMBOYANT AS THE CAPED CRUSADER'S LATER MOTORCYCLE, THE ORIGINAL BIKE WAS STILL AN IMPRESSIVE MACHINE.

Following its debut in 1966, the classic Batman TV series took the world by storm – every episode seemingly exploding with novel ideas and innovative storytelling techniques. The show's action-filled plots and colorful set pieces captivated younger viewers, while its wry, self-aware humor appealed to teenagers and adults on a wholly different level.

The original Batcycle was an integral part of the first season episode "Not Yet, He Ain't." As stylish as the ubiquitous Batmobile, the bike was a thrilling addition to the TV canon.

While it had the appearance of an ordinary bike, the Batcycle was anything but a regular ride. It was a gadget-laden wonder that elicited both amazement and amusement from the audience.

When the Penguin stole the Batmobile, the Dynamic Duo gave chase on the Batcycle. From the sidecar, Robin observed, "Time to jolt him with our gimmicks!" Batman concurred, using the Batcycle's remote-control circuitry to activate the Batmobile's ejector seats – propelling the Penguin's henchmen into the air.

THE BRITISH BATMOBILE IN ACTION!

Hats off

The Batcycle was just one of Batman's many vehicles. The Caped Crusader was ready for crime to strike in any part of the world, with a London taxi-cab converted to a Batmobile just in case he was called into action across the pond. Such foresight was indeed fortuitous, as the Mad Hatter took a supposed vacation to the United Kingdom but only in order to steal the Crown Jewels. The Dynamic Duo were already hot on the villain's heels, however, and brought him to book with a blast from the British Batmobile's laser beam.

> COME ON, ALFRED, I'M GOING TO NEED YOUR ENCYCLOPEDIC KNOWLEDGE OF LONDON'S STREETS!

> I AM CONVINCED THAT HATTER HAS A TECHNICAL-MINDED ACCOMPLICE.

> SOMEONE WHO WAS SIGNALING HIM FROM THE CLOCK TOWER TO STAY AWAY AND NOT COME HERE.

FIRST APPEARANCE

The Caped Crusader's original Batcycle appeared only once on the small screen – in the concluding chapter of a two-part adventure that featured the Penguin adopting fresh plumage to become Batman's crime-fighting rival.

In "The Penguin Goes Straight," the waddling felon saved Sophia Starr – the so-called Beauteous Queen of Gotham City Society – from a masked jewelry thief. The apparently reformed villain went on to establish The Penguin Protective Agency, Inc – a P.I. agency dedicated to defending the great and the good of Gotham City from hoodlums. Naturally, Batman was suspicious of the Penguin's motives. Even more so when the Penguin announced his intention to marry Sophia Starr. Batman believed his foe was after Miss Starr's collection of priceless jewelry, and so it proved to be...

THE ORIGINAL BATCYCLE WAS A TRUE TRAILBLAZER. IT WAS A HIGHLY MANEUVERABLE MACHINE THAT RACED TOWARDS DANGER AND LED THE WAY FOR AN EVEN MORE AWESOME MOTORCYCLE.

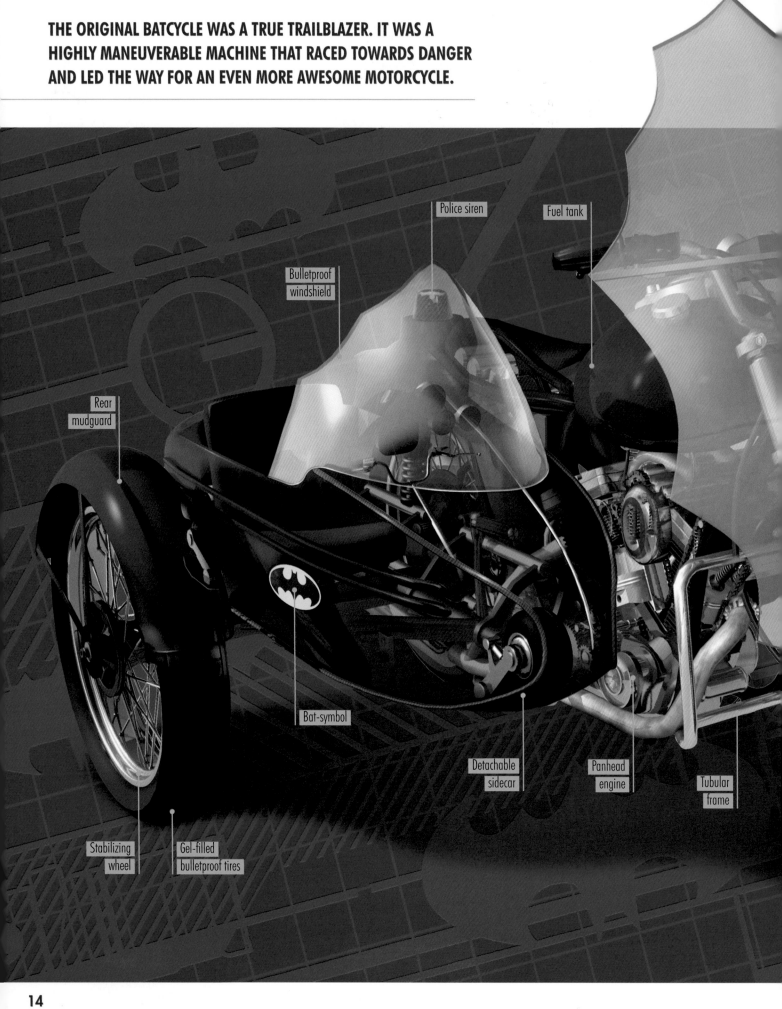

Police siren

Fuel tank

Bulletproof windshield

Rear mudguard

Bat-symbol

Detachable sidecar

Panhead engine

Tubular frame

Stabilizing wheel

Gel-filled bulletproof tires

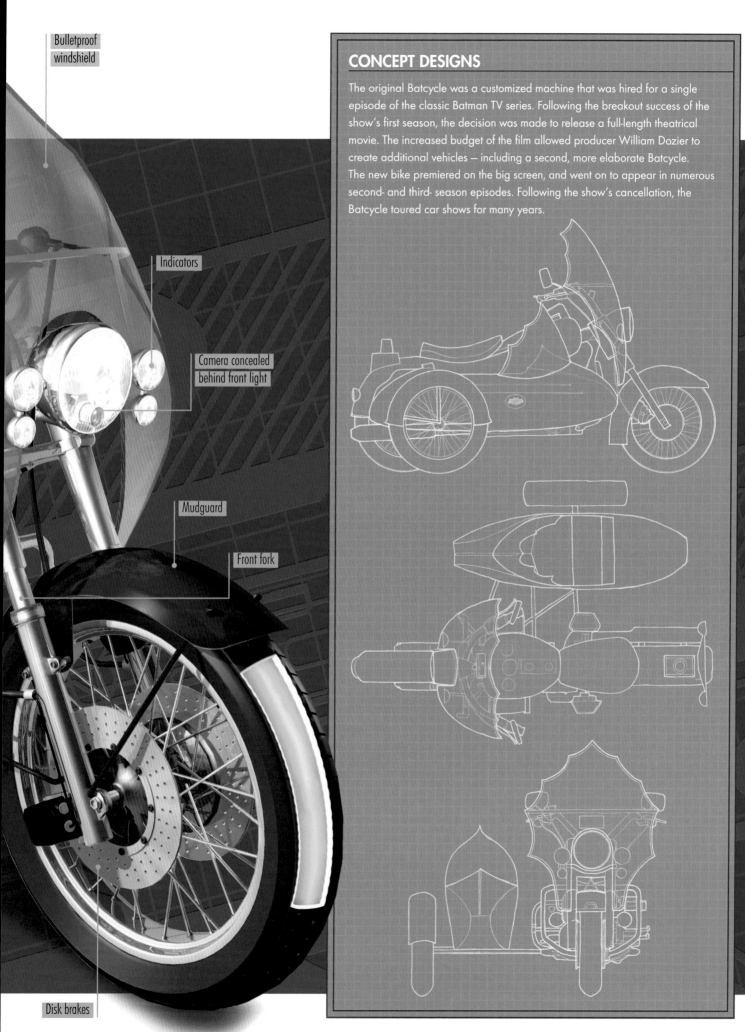

Bulletproof
windshield

Indicators

Camera concealed
behind front light

Mudguard

Front fork

Disk brakes

CONCEPT DESIGNS

The original Batcycle was a customized machine that was hired for a single episode of the classic Batman TV series. Following the breakout success of the show's first season, the decision was made to release a full-length theatrical movie. The increased budget of the film allowed producer William Dozier to create additional vehicles — including a second, more elaborate Batcycle. The new bike premiered on the big screen, and went on to appear in numerous second- and third- season episodes. Following the show's cancellation, the Batcycle toured car shows for many years.

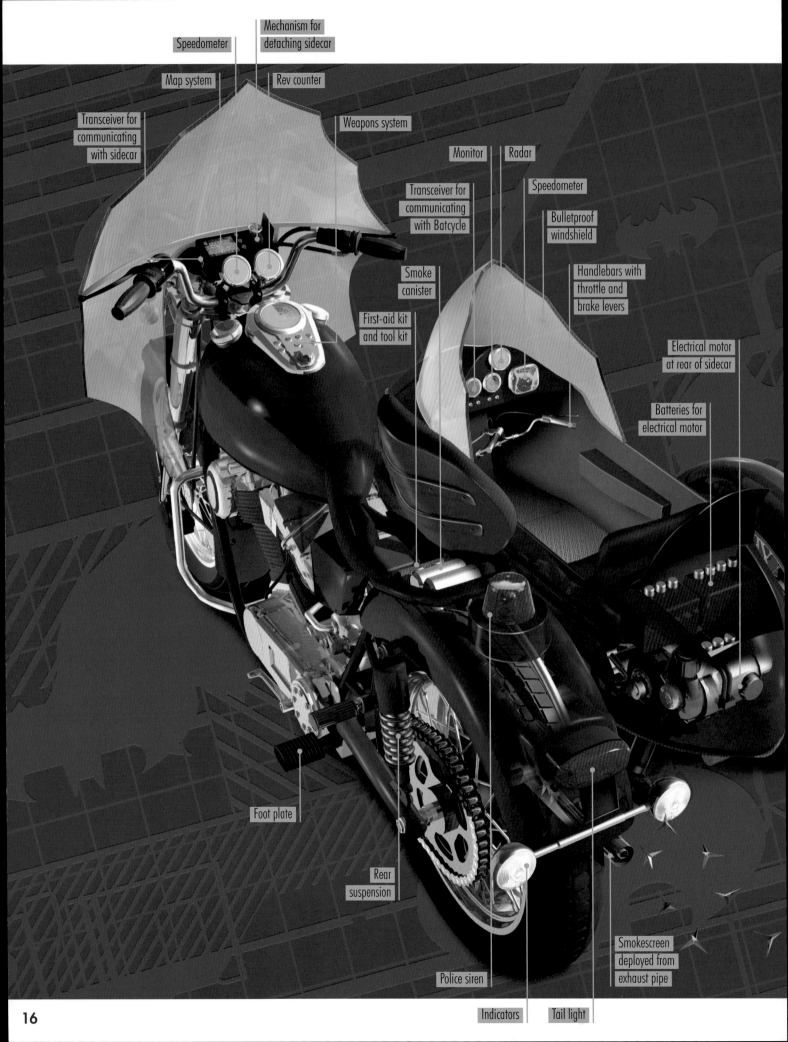

Speedometer

Mechanism for detaching sidecar

Map system

Rev counter

Transceiver for communicating with sidecar

Weapons system

Monitor

Radar

Speedometer

Transceiver for communicating with Batcycle

Bulletproof windshield

Smoke canister

Handlebars with throttle and brake levers

First-aid kit and tool kit

Electrical motor at rear of sidecar

Batteries for electrical motor

Foot plate

Rear suspension

Police siren

Smokescreen deployed from exhaust pipe

Indicators

Tail light

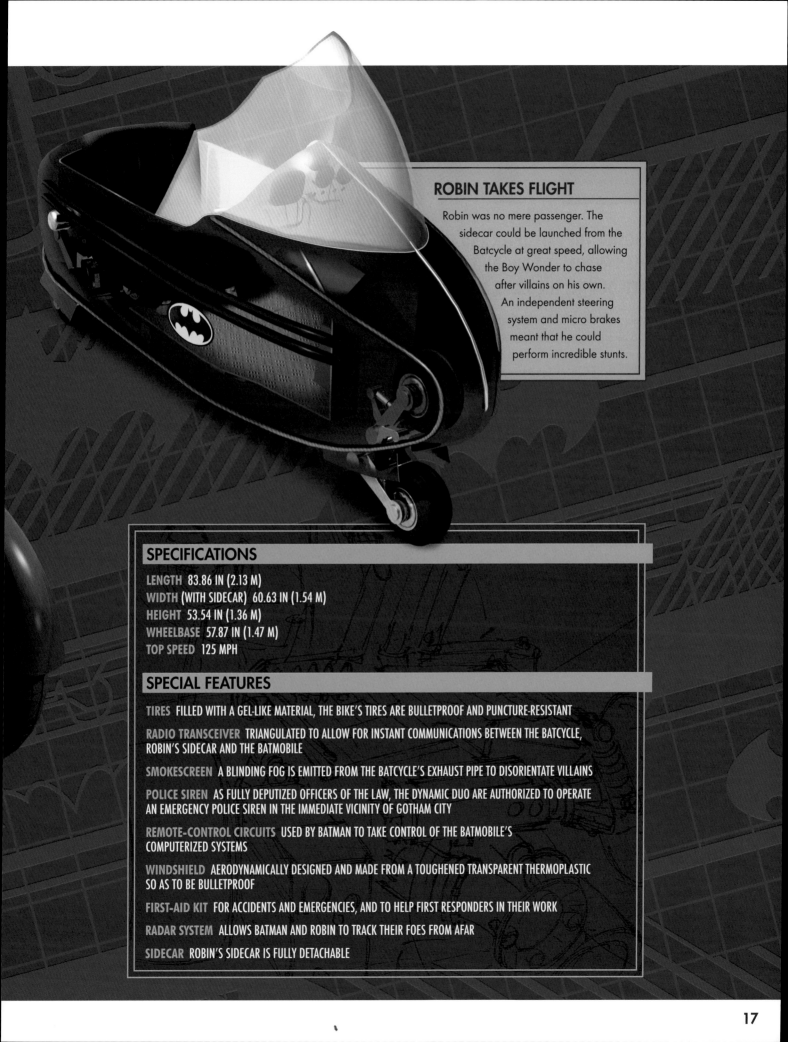

ROBIN TAKES FLIGHT

Robin was no mere passenger. The sidecar could be launched from the Batcycle at great speed, allowing the Boy Wonder to chase after villains on his own. An independent steering system and micro brakes meant that he could perform incredible stunts.

SPECIFICATIONS

LENGTH 83.86 IN (2.13 M)
WIDTH (WITH SIDECAR) 60.63 IN (1.54 M)
HEIGHT 53.54 IN (1.36 M)
WHEELBASE 57.87 IN (1.47 M)
TOP SPEED 125 MPH

SPECIAL FEATURES

TIRES FILLED WITH A GEL-LIKE MATERIAL, THE BIKE'S TIRES ARE BULLETPROOF AND PUNCTURE-RESISTANT

RADIO TRANSCEIVER TRIANGULATED TO ALLOW FOR INSTANT COMMUNICATIONS BETWEEN THE BATCYCLE, ROBIN'S SIDECAR AND THE BATMOBILE

SMOKESCREEN A BLINDING FOG IS EMITTED FROM THE BATCYCLE'S EXHAUST PIPE TO DISORIENTATE VILLAINS

POLICE SIREN AS FULLY DEPUTIZED OFFICERS OF THE LAW, THE DYNAMIC DUO ARE AUTHORIZED TO OPERATE AN EMERGENCY POLICE SIREN IN THE IMMEDIATE VICINITY OF GOTHAM CITY

REMOTE-CONTROL CIRCUITS USED BY BATMAN TO TAKE CONTROL OF THE BATMOBILE'S COMPUTERIZED SYSTEMS

WINDSHIELD AERODYNAMICALLY DESIGNED AND MADE FROM A TOUGHENED TRANSPARENT THERMOPLASTIC SO AS TO BE BULLETPROOF

FIRST-AID KIT FOR ACCIDENTS AND EMERGENCIES, AND TO HELP FIRST RESPONDERS IN THEIR WORK

RADAR SYSTEM ALLOWS BATMAN AND ROBIN TO TRACK THEIR FOES FROM AFAR

SIDECAR ROBIN'S SIDECAR IS FULLY DETACHABLE

RACE AGAINST TIME

ALONGSIDE THE BATCOPTER AND THE BATBOAT, THE BATCYCLE DEBUTED IN THE 1966 BATMAN MOVIE — A BIG-BUDGET EXTRAVAGANZA IN WHICH THE CAPED CRUSADER PULLED OUT ALL THE STOPS, USING EVERYTHING IN HIS CRIME-FIGHTING ARSENAL.

There were two Batcycles featured in the classic Batman TV series. The original version appeared on screen only once, in the first-season episode "Not Yet, He Ain't." In that story, Batman and Robin used a Batman-themed bike and sidecar to race after the Penguin, who was making a hasty getaway in the Batmobile. Some months later, in the 1966 Batman movie, the new Batcycle was unveiled — literally — as the Caped Crusader suddenly pulled back some camouflage netting to reveal the sleek speedster in all its glory. The Penguin had purloined the Batmobile for a second time, and so the Dynamic Duo gave chase once again, with Batman cornering the Batcycle at breakneck speeds and Robin hugging the ground in a monogrammed sidecar.

The Batcycle sped into an airfield, with Robin's sidecar splitting off to form a separate go-kart. The Boy Wonder's kart screeched to a halt at the passenger side of the Batcopter, and Batman leapt from the Batcycle to take the controls of the whirlybird. The Batcopter was soon airborne, and the Dynamic Duo continued to chase their prey from on high.

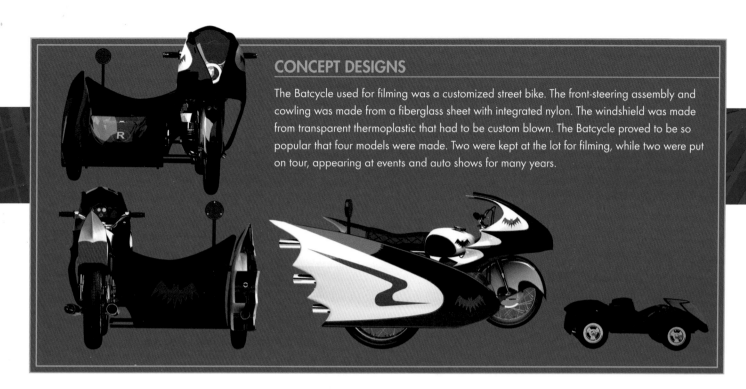

CONCEPT DESIGNS

The Batcycle used for filming was a customized street bike. The front-steering assembly and cowling was made from a fiberglass sheet with integrated nylon. The windshield was made from transparent thermoplastic that had to be custom blown. The Batcycle proved to be so popular that four models were made. Two were kept at the lot for filming, while two were put on tour, appearing at events and auto shows for many years.

BATTERING RAM

THE BATCYCLE WAS DESIGNED TO TAKE BATMAN AND ROBIN INTO PLACES THAT THE BATMOBILE JUST COULDN'T GO. IT WAS HIGHLY MANEUVERABLE AND ALLOWED THE DYNAMIC DUO TO RACE RIGHT TO THE HEART OF THE ACTION.

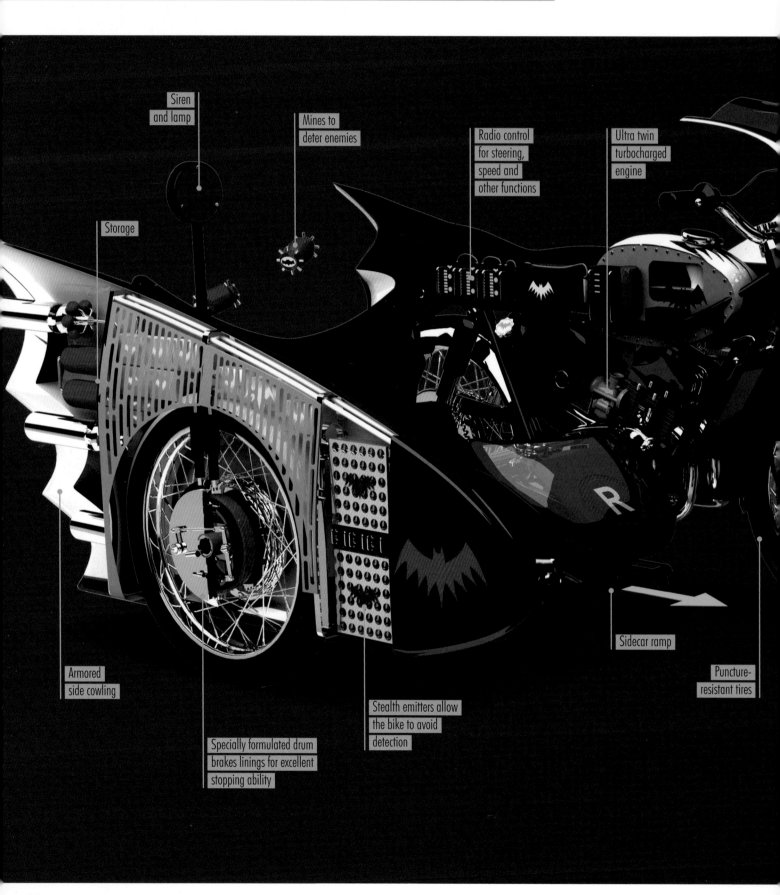

Siren and lamp

Mines to deter enemies

Radio control for steering, speed and other functions

Ultra twin turbocharged engine

Storage

Sidecar ramp

Armored side cowling

Puncture-resistant tires

Stealth emitters allow the bike to avoid detection

Specially formulated drum brakes linings for excellent stopping ability

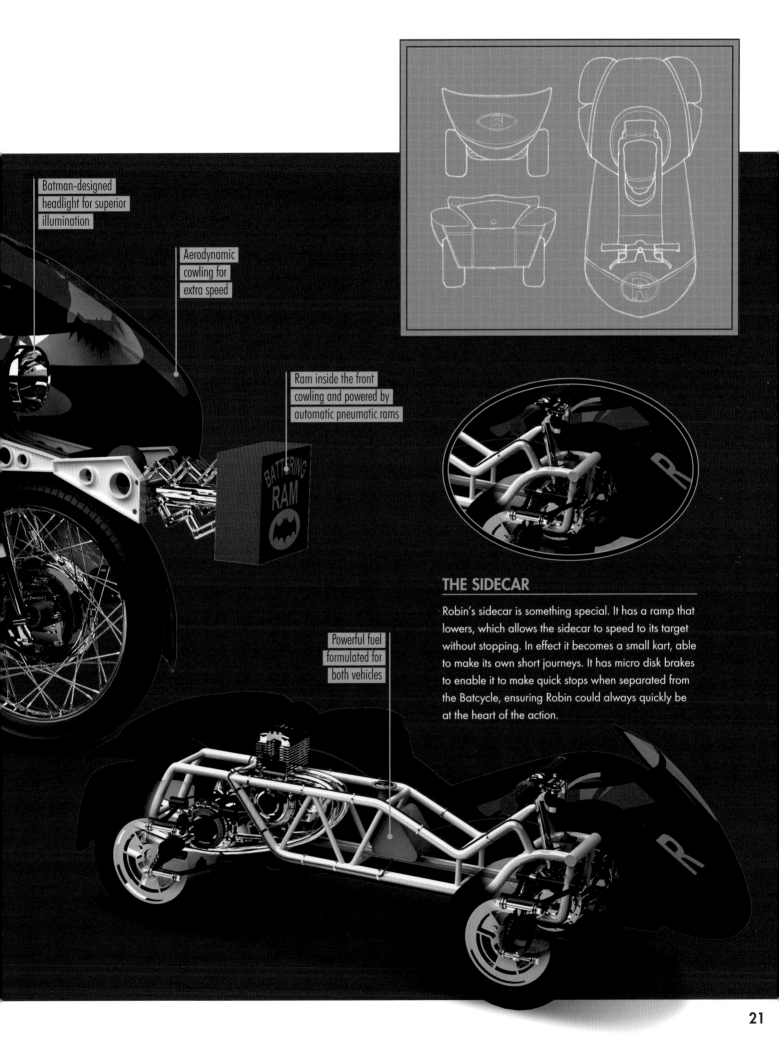

Batman-designed headlight for superior illumination

Aerodynamic cowling for extra speed

Ram inside the front cowling and powered by automatic pneumatic rams

BATTERING RAM

Powerful fuel formulated for both vehicles

THE SIDECAR

Robin's sidecar is something special. It has a ramp that lowers, which allows the sidecar to speed to its target without stopping. In effect it becomes a small kart, able to make its own short journeys. It has micro disk brakes to enable it to make quick stops when separated from the Batcycle, ensuring Robin could always quickly be at the heart of the action.

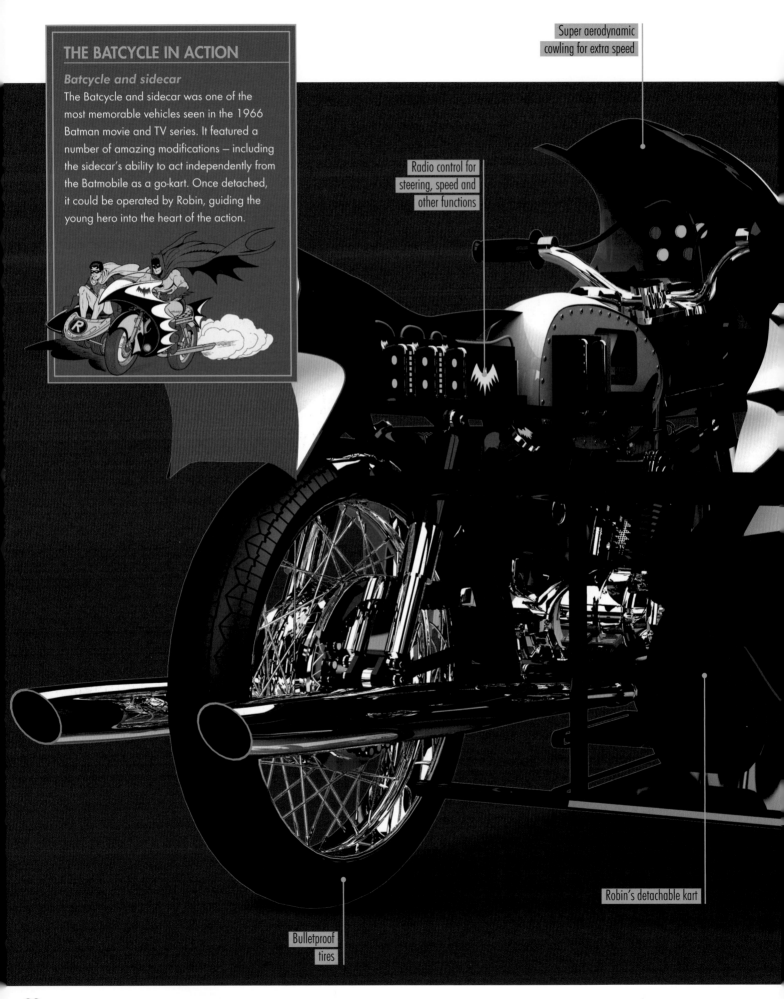

THE BATCYCLE IN ACTION

Batcycle and sidecar

The Batcycle and sidecar was one of the most memorable vehicles seen in the 1966 Batman movie and TV series. It featured a number of amazing modifications — including the sidecar's ability to act independently from the Batmobile as a go-kart. Once detached, it could be operated by Robin, guiding the young hero into the heart of the action.

Super aerodynamic cowling for extra speed

Radio control for steering, speed and other functions

Robin's detachable kart

Bulletproof tires

Siren and lamp

Rocket assist to boost acceleration

Special mines to deter enemies

Armored side cowling

BATTERING RAM

The stylish battering ram can be pushed out from the front of the bike at the touch of a button for maximum effect. Its pneumatic construction enables it to be put into action with exceptional speed. Constructed with ultra-strong steel, it can withstand impact into walls and other vehicles without risking damage to the rider. It proved to be an essential accessory on the Batcycle for the Caped Crusader.

BATTERING RAM

SPECIFICATIONS

LENGTH 111.7 IN (2.84M)
WIDTH 81.6 IN (2.07 M)
WHEELBASE 65.26 IN (1.66 M)
HEIGHT 62.9 IN (1.6 M)
WHEEL WIDTH (FRONT) 5.18 IN (1.32 M)
WHEEL WIDTH (REAR) 5.6 IN (1.43 M)

SPECIAL FEATURES

BATTERING RAM THE HIGHLY STYLIZED BATTERING RAM IS HIDDEN INSIDE THE FRONT COWLING AND IS POWERED BY AUTOMATIC PNEUMATIC RAMS

RADIO CONTROL THE ADVANCED RADIO-CONTROL SYSTEM PROVIDES BATMAN AND ROBIN WITH THE ABILITY TO OPERATE THE BIKE REMOTELY

ARMOR THE SIDE AND FRONT COWLING IS ARMORED FOR EXTRA PROTECTION

ENGINE POWERED BY TWIN TURBOCHARGED ENGINES WHICH USES NEWLY DEVELOPED FUEL FOR MAXIMUM EFFECT

BULLETPROOF TIRES SPECIAL BULLETPROOF TIRES PROVIDE ADDED PROTECTION FROM BULLETS AND TRAPS

SIDECAR THE SIDECAR IS DETACHABLE AND CAN OPERATE FOR SHORT PERIODS ON ITS OWN

BAT MINES THE REAR OF THE BIKE CAN DISCHARGE SPECIAL MINES THAT CAN SLOW DOWN ANY PURSUERS

STEALTH EMITTERS THE BATCYCLE'S STEALTH EMITTERS ALLOW THE BIKE TO TRAVEL IN SECRET, WITHOUT RADAR PICKING UP ITS MOVEMENT

HEADLIGHTS POWERFUL HEADLIGHTS ESPECIALLY DESIGNED TO STARTLE ENEMIES AND PROVIDE MAXIMUM ILLUMINATION

MAKING A
SPLASH

BATS MAY BE MORE AT HOME IN THE AIR THAN IN THE SEA, BUT THAT DIDN'T DETER THE CAPED CRUSADER FROM LAUNCHING HIS VERY OWN BATBOAT. THIS IMPRESSIVE VESSEL WAS A HIGH-SPEED ADDITION TO THE DARK KNIGHT'S ARMORY.

The Batboat made its debut in the 1966 Batman movie, in which Batman and Robin investigated the mysterious disappearance of Commodore Schmidlapp, whose seafaring yacht had failed to make port in Gotham City. With a cry of "To the Batboat — fast!" Batman led Robin to an oceanside wharf where the sleek powerboat was moored, seemingly just waiting to be put through her paces.

The Dynamic Duo soon uncovered a criminal conspiracy by the Joker, Catwoman, the Penguin and the Riddler, all planning to use Commodore Schmidlapp's dehydrator device to extort billions from the world's richest nations. As the movie sailed towards the finish line, the heroes confronted the villains on the high seas, using the Batboat to storm the Penguin's high-powered submarine.

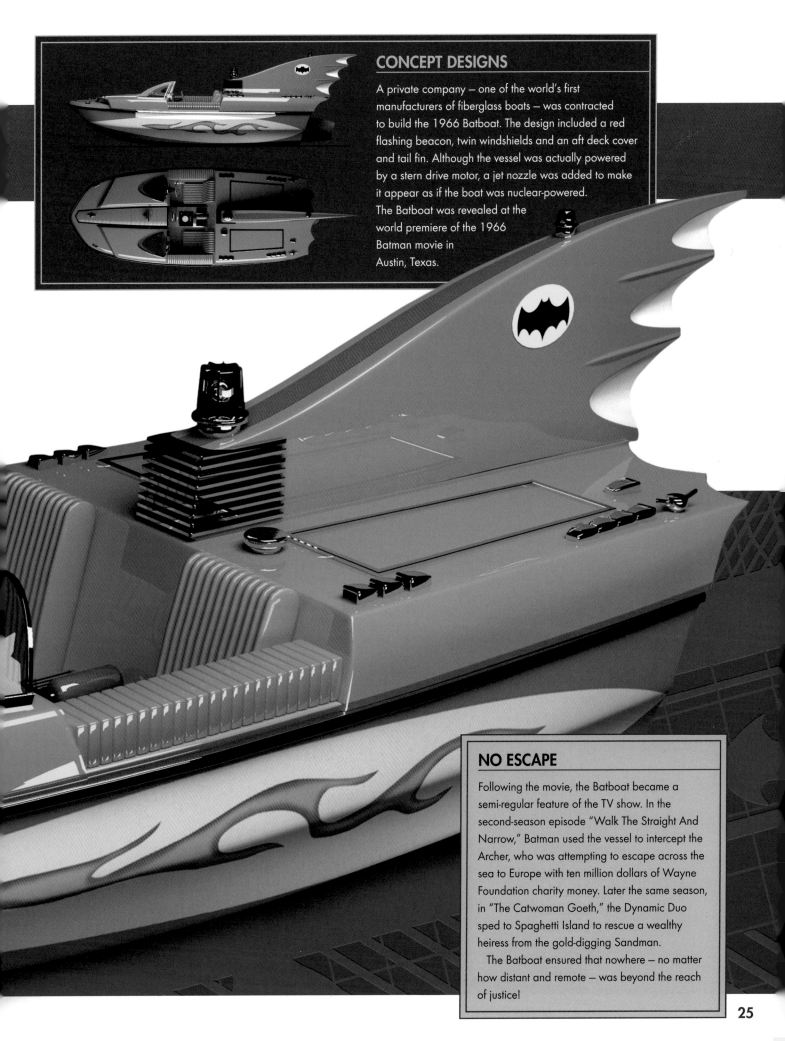

CONCEPT DESIGNS

A private company — one of the world's first manufacturers of fiberglass boats — was contracted to build the 1966 Batboat. The design included a red flashing beacon, twin windshields and an aft deck cover and tail fin. Although the vessel was actually powered by a stern drive motor, a jet nozzle was added to make it appear as if the boat was nuclear-powered. The Batboat was revealed at the world premiere of the 1966 Batman movie in Austin, Texas.

NO ESCAPE

Following the movie, the Batboat became a semi-regular feature of the TV show. In the second-season episode "Walk The Straight And Narrow," Batman used the vessel to intercept the Archer, who was attempting to escape across the sea to Europe with ten million dollars of Wayne Foundation charity money. Later the same season, in "The Catwoman Goeth," the Dynamic Duo sped to Spaghetti Island to rescue a wealthy heiress from the gold-digging Sandman.

The Batboat ensured that nowhere — no matter how distant and remote — was beyond the reach of justice!

25

THE 1966 BATBOAT WAS DESIGNED TO BE IMPRESSIVE.
IT WAS A HIGH-TECH OCEAN BEAST THAT MADE WAVES
FROM THE FIRST MOMENT OF ITS MOVIE DEBUT IN THE
BIG-SCREEN SPIN-OFF FROM THE CLASSIC TV SHOW.

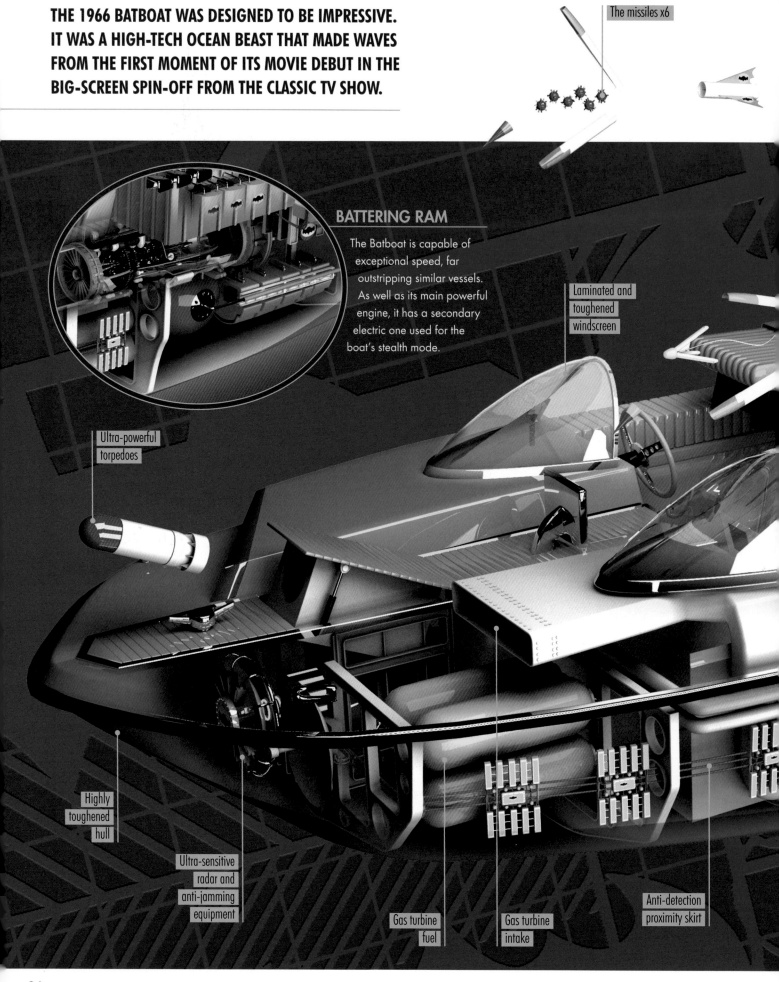

The missiles x6

BATTERING RAM

The Batboat is capable of
exceptional speed, far
outstripping similar vessels.
As well as its main powerful
engine, it has a secondary
electric one used for the
boat's stealth mode.

Laminated and
toughened
windscreen

Ultra-powerful
torpedoes

Highly
toughened
hull

Ultra-sensitive
radar and
anti-jamming
equipment

Gas turbine
fuel

Gas turbine
intake

Anti-detection
proximity skirt

26

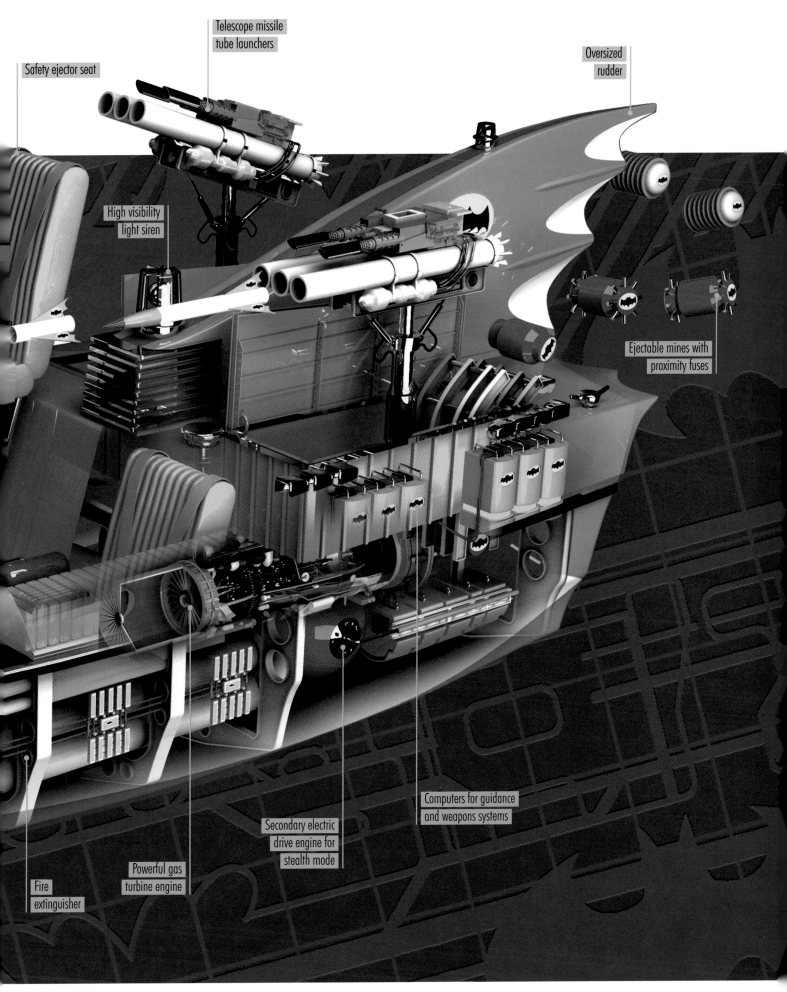

Safety ejector seat

Telescope missile tube launchers

Oversized rudder

High visibility light siren

Ejectable mines with proximity fuses

Computers for guidance and weapons systems

Secondary electric drive engine for stealth mode

Powerful gas turbine engine

Fire extinguisher

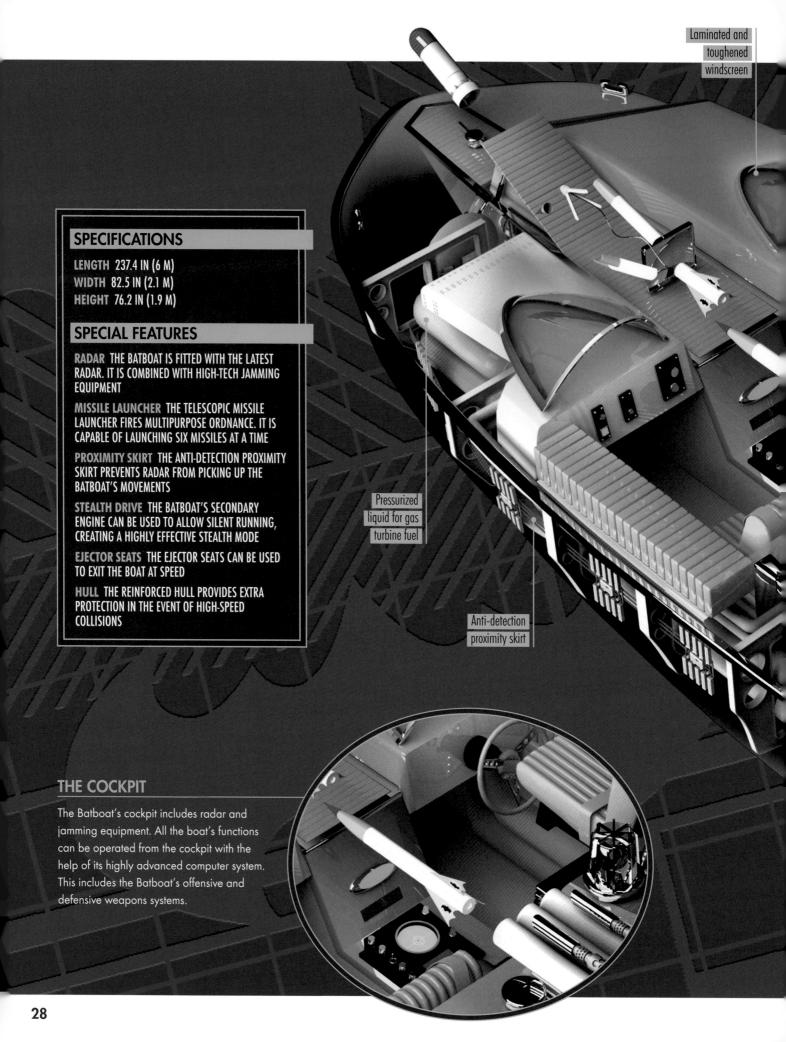

SPECIFICATIONS

LENGTH 237.4 IN (6 M)
WIDTH 82.5 IN (2.1 M)
HEIGHT 76.2 IN (1.9 M)

SPECIAL FEATURES

RADAR THE BATBOAT IS FITTED WITH THE LATEST RADAR. IT IS COMBINED WITH HIGH-TECH JAMMING EQUIPMENT

MISSILE LAUNCHER THE TELESCOPIC MISSILE LAUNCHER FIRES MULTIPURPOSE ORDNANCE. IT IS CAPABLE OF LAUNCHING SIX MISSILES AT A TIME

PROXIMITY SKIRT THE ANTI-DETECTION PROXIMITY SKIRT PREVENTS RADAR FROM PICKING UP THE BATBOAT'S MOVEMENTS

STEALTH DRIVE THE BATBOAT'S SECONDARY ENGINE CAN BE USED TO ALLOW SILENT RUNNING, CREATING A HIGHLY EFFECTIVE STEALTH MODE

EJECTOR SEATS THE EJECTOR SEATS CAN BE USED TO EXIT THE BOAT AT SPEED

HULL THE REINFORCED HULL PROVIDES EXTRA PROTECTION IN THE EVENT OF HIGH-SPEED COLLISIONS

Pressurized liquid for gas turbine fuel

Anti-detection proximity skirt

THE COCKPIT

The Batboat's cockpit includes radar and jamming equipment. All the boat's functions can be operated from the cockpit with the help of its highly advanced computer system. This includes the Batboat's offensive and defensive weapons systems.

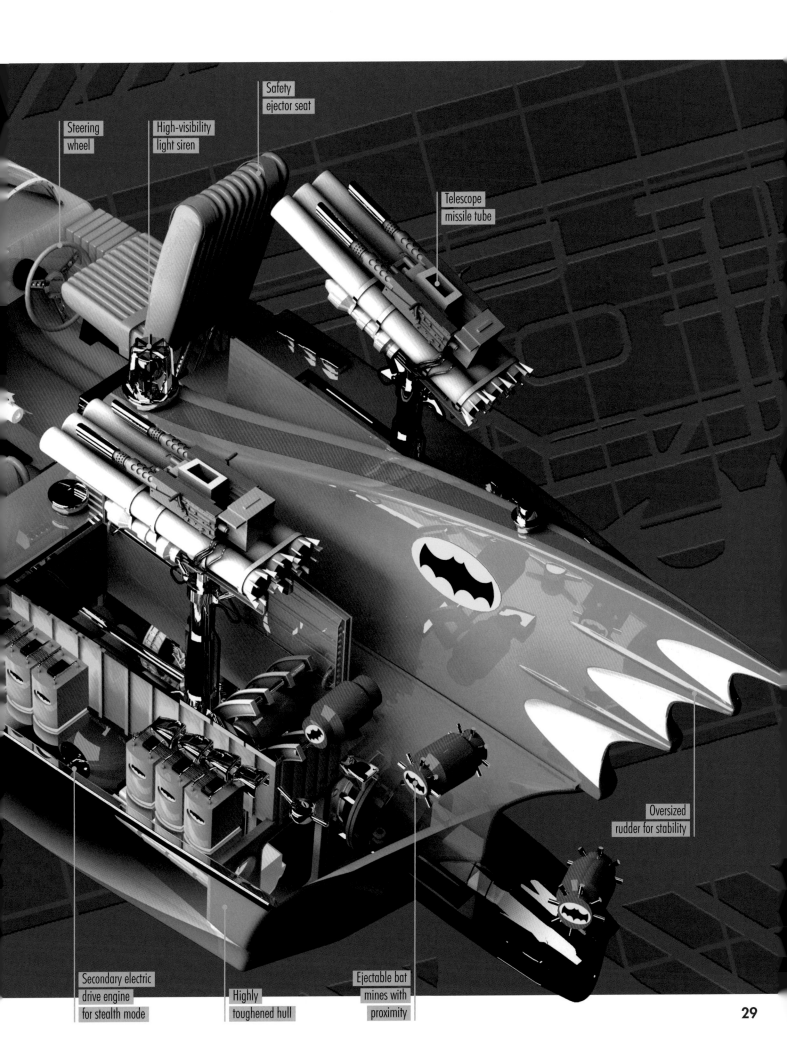

Steering
wheel

High-visibility
light siren

Safety
ejector seat

Telescope
missile tube

Oversized
rudder for stability

Secondary electric
drive engine
for stealth mode

Highly
toughened hull

Ejectable bat
mines with
proximity

CRIME-FIGHTING COPTER

THE BATCOPTER WAS A TOP-FLIGHT ADDITION TO BATMAN'S CRIME-FIGHTING ARSENAL, STIRRING UP A STORM IN THE 1966 BATMAN MOVIE BEFORE BECOMING A REGULAR FEATURE OF THE CLASSIC BATMAN TV SERIES.

The Batcopter was kept fueled and ready for take-off at all times. In the 1966 Batman movie, this meant that the Dynamic Duo could instantly fly out to sea to investigate a threat to Commodore Schmidlapp's luxury ocean liner. Later, Batman took to the skies to track the Penguin to a secret submersible that the villain was sharing with his cohorts in crime – the Joker, Catwoman and the Riddler.

Following the movie, the Batcopter became a semi-regular feature of the TV show. In the second-season episode "A Riddling Controversy", Batman used the Batcopter to seed the clouds with a dichloride compound. This produced a lightning bolt that destroyed a Demoleculariser device that the Riddler was using to threaten Police HQ.

With renewed interest in the classic Batman TV series, the Batcopter was featured in the third issue of Batman '66 – a monthly comic launched in 2013 to showcase new stories set within the madcap milieu of the show. Dropped from a great height by the "egg-centric" Egghead, Batman and Robin summoned the Batcopter via remote control. They scrambled aboard the still-moving whirlybird and proceeded to force down the villain's Egg Zeppelin.

CONCEPT DESIGNS

Like the Batboat and the Batcycle that debuted alongside it, the Batcopter was a fully functioning vehicle customized by the Batman movie production team. It was leased from the National Helicopter Service and made to look more like a super hero craft with the addition of red canvas-covered tubular frames and a bat-symbol painted to the windshield. The most extensive revision was the addition of wings – which reduced the helicopter's power by nearly fifty percent. For the scenes at sea, the Batcopter was filmed off the coast of Palos Verdes, California, while Van Nuys Airport was used to shoot footage of the chopper taking off.

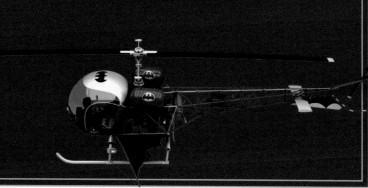

FIRST APPEARANCE

Produced by William Dozier and directed by Leslie H. Martinson, *Batman* was a big-budget extravaganza that overflowed with outrageous action sequences. The Batcopter took to the skies for the first time early on in the proceedings. Discovering that Commodore Schmidlapp – the inventor of an amazing dehydrator machine – was in danger of kidnap, the Dynamic Duo used the whirlybird to launch a rescue mission. They flew out to meet the Commodore's yacht as it was about to make port in Gotham City. Without warning, however, the yacht vanished inexplicably... and the Caped Crusader found himself in a deadly confrontation with a man-eating shark. Robin came to the rescue with one of the many oceanic repellent sprays stored in the chopper's cockpit. The repellent saw off the shark – which then exploded, having been booby-trapped by the mysterious villains responsible for the Commodore's disappearance.

THE BATCOPTER WAS A HIGHLY MANEUVERABLE PURSUIT VEHICLE THAT GAVE BATMAN AND ROBIN EYES AND EARS IN THE AIR. IT CAUSED A STIR FROM THE FIRST MOMENT OF ITS DRAMATIC BIG-SCREEN DEBUT.

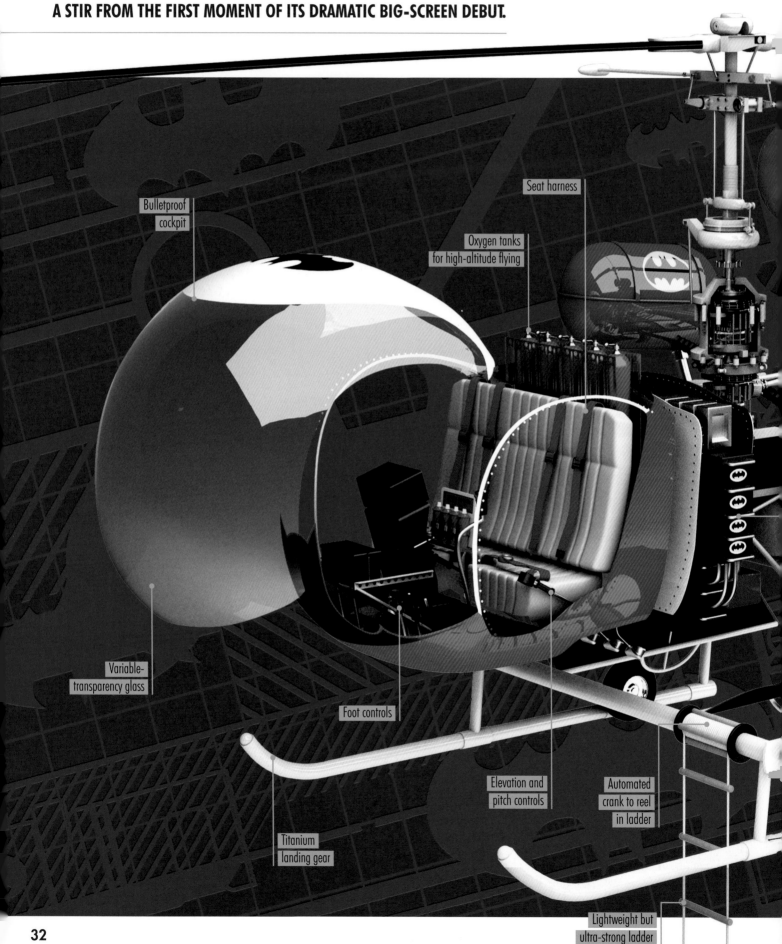

Bulletproof cockpit

Seat harness

Oxygen tanks for high-altitude flying

Variable-transparency glass

Foot controls

Titanium landing gear

Elevation and pitch controls

Automated crank to reel in ladder

Lightweight but ultra-strong ladder

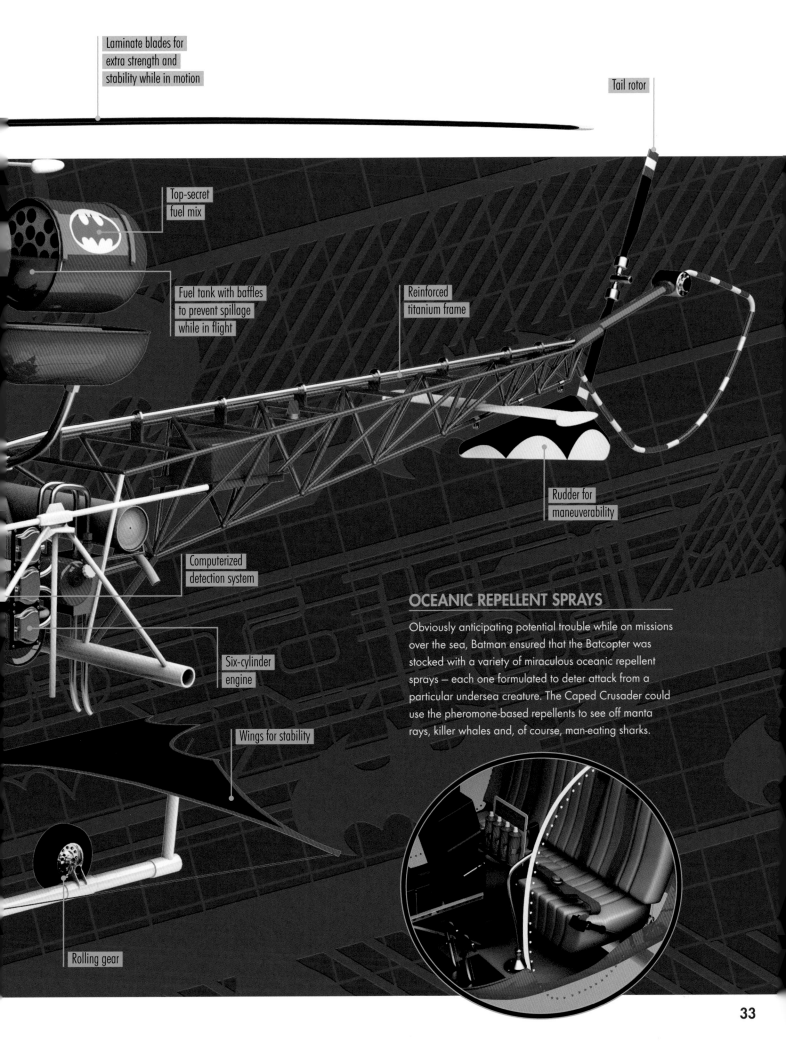

Laminate blades for extra strength and stability while in motion

Tail rotor

Top-secret fuel mix

Fuel tank with baffles to prevent spillage while in flight

Reinforced titanium frame

Rudder for maneuverability

Computerized detection system

OCEANIC REPELLENT SPRAYS

Obviously anticipating potential trouble while on missions over the sea, Batman ensured that the Batcopter was stocked with a variety of miraculous oceanic repellent sprays — each one formulated to deter attack from a particular undersea creature. The Caped Crusader could use the pheromone-based repellents to see off manta rays, killer whales and, of course, man-eating sharks.

Six-cylinder engine

Wings for stability

Rolling gear

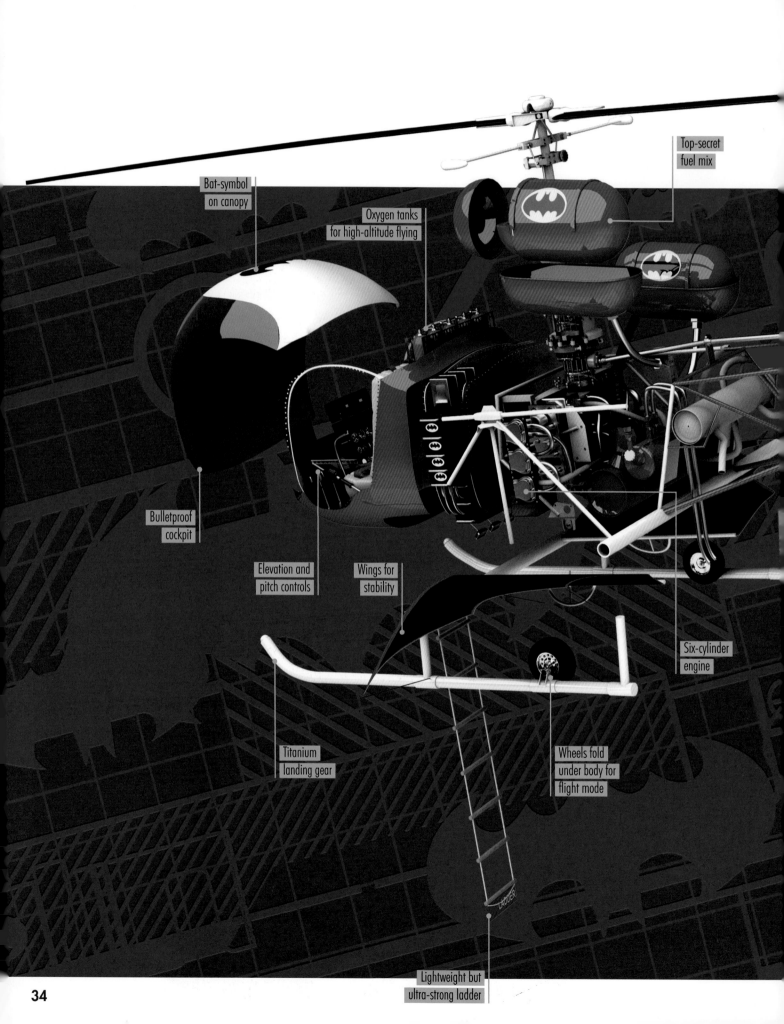

Bat-symbol
on canopy

Oxygen tanks
for high-altitude flying

Top-secret
fuel mix

Bulletproof
cockpit

Elevation and
pitch controls

Wings for
stability

Six-cylinder
engine

Titanium
landing gear

Wheels fold
under body for
flight mode

Lightweight but
ultra-strong ladder

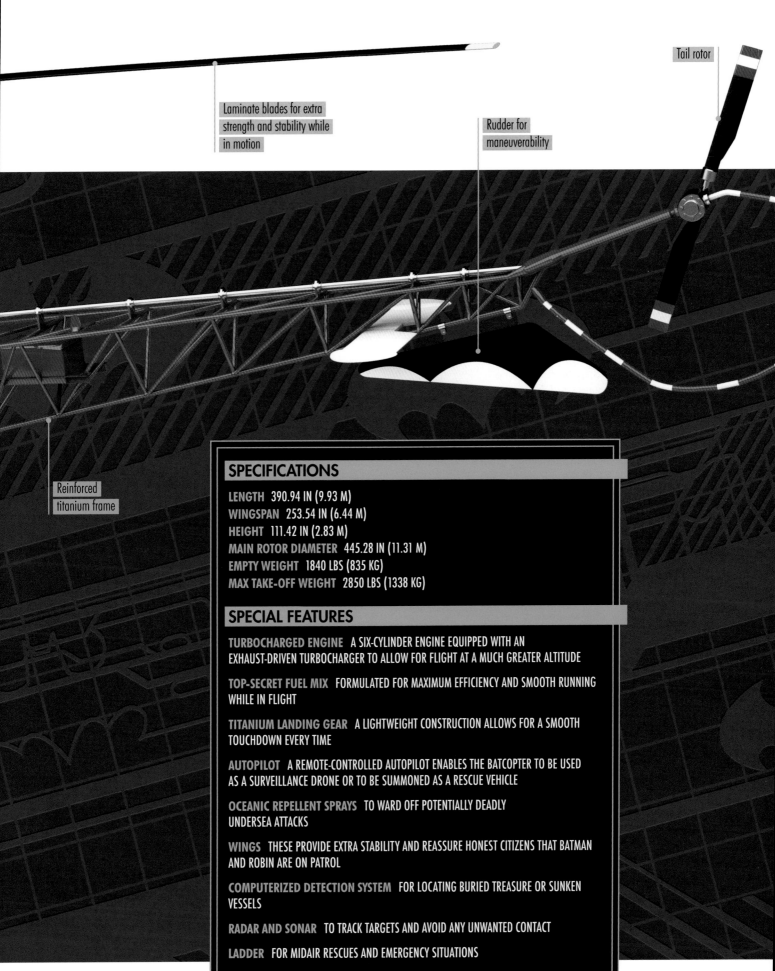

Laminate blades for extra strength and stability while in motion

Rudder for maneuverability

Tail rotor

Reinforced titanium frame

SPECIFICATIONS

LENGTH 390.94 IN (9.93 M)
WINGSPAN 253.54 IN (6.44 M)
HEIGHT 111.42 IN (2.83 M)
MAIN ROTOR DIAMETER 445.28 IN (11.31 M)
EMPTY WEIGHT 1840 LBS (835 KG)
MAX TAKE-OFF WEIGHT 2850 LBS (1338 KG)

SPECIAL FEATURES

TURBOCHARGED ENGINE A SIX-CYLINDER ENGINE EQUIPPED WITH AN EXHAUST-DRIVEN TURBOCHARGER TO ALLOW FOR FLIGHT AT A MUCH GREATER ALTITUDE

TOP-SECRET FUEL MIX FORMULATED FOR MAXIMUM EFFICIENCY AND SMOOTH RUNNING WHILE IN FLIGHT

TITANIUM LANDING GEAR A LIGHTWEIGHT CONSTRUCTION ALLOWS FOR A SMOOTH TOUCHDOWN EVERY TIME

AUTOPILOT A REMOTE-CONTROLLED AUTOPILOT ENABLES THE BATCOPTER TO BE USED AS A SURVEILLANCE DRONE OR TO BE SUMMONED AS A RESCUE VEHICLE

OCEANIC REPELLENT SPRAYS TO WARD OFF POTENTIALLY DEADLY UNDERSEA ATTACKS

WINGS THESE PROVIDE EXTRA STABILITY AND REASSURE HONEST CITIZENS THAT BATMAN AND ROBIN ARE ON PATROL

COMPUTERIZED DETECTION SYSTEM FOR LOCATING BURIED TREASURE OR SUNKEN VESSELS

RADAR AND SONAR TO TRACK TARGETS AND AVOID ANY UNWANTED CONTACT

LADDER FOR MIDAIR RESCUES AND EMERGENCY SITUATIONS

PURPLE RIDE

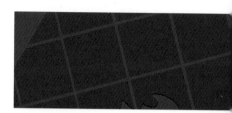

THE CLASSIC BATMAN TV SERIES HAD TAKEN THE WORLD BY STORM — CAPTURING FANS YOUNG AND OLD ALIKE. KEEPING THINGS FRESH, PRODUCER WILLIAM DOZIER ADDED THE CHARACTER OF BATGIRL TO THE MIX IN SEPTEMBER 1967.

Batgirl made her small-screen debut in the third season of the classic Batman TV show. Librarian Barbara Gordon was secretly Batgirl and her commitment to combating Gotham City's crime was as strong as that of the Dynamic Duo — and she had the crime-fighting toys to prove it! The Batgirl Cycle was kept in a secret storage room in Barbara's trendy Park Ridge apartment. The bike was accessed through a mechanical iris, and Batgirl would use a long-abandoned freight elevator to take it down to street level. There she would burst through a fake brick wall and roar into the night in search of nefarious wrongdoers.

The Batgirl Cycle was a mini-Batcave on wheels. It contained everything needed to investigate a robbery or hunt the likes of the Penguin and the Joker. In the episode "How to Hatch a Dinosaur," Batgirl used the cycle's inbuilt Geiger counter to locate a small quantity of radium that had been stolen by Egghead, reaching the villain's secret headquarters at exactly the same time as a bemused Batman and Robin.

Batgirl was a tough and independent heroine, and the Batgirl Cycle ensured that she blazed a trail that others were sure to follow.

THE BATGIRL CYCLE IN ACTION

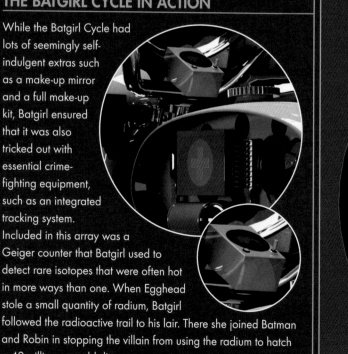

While the Batgirl Cycle had lots of seemingly self-indulgent extras such as a make-up mirror and a full make-up kit, Batgirl ensured that it was also tricked out with essential crime-fighting equipment, such as an integrated tracking system. Included in this array was a Geiger counter that Batgirl used to detect rare isotopes that were often hot in more ways than one. When Egghead stole a small quantity of radium, Batgirl followed the radioactive trail to his lair. There she joined Batman and Robin in stopping the villain from using the radium to hatch a 40-million-year-old dinosaur egg.

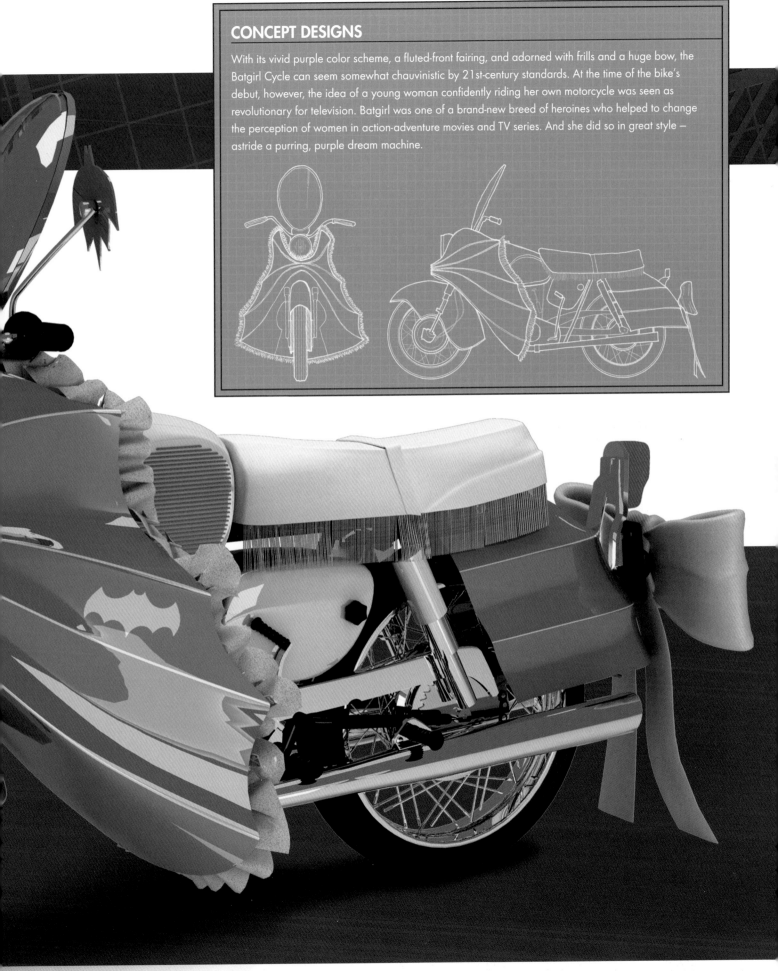

CONCEPT DESIGNS

With its vivid purple color scheme, a fluted-front fairing, and adorned with frills and a huge bow, the Batgirl Cycle can seem somewhat chauvinistic by 21st-century standards. At the time of the bike's debut, however, the idea of a young woman confidently riding her own motorcycle was seen as revolutionary for television. Batgirl was one of a brand-new breed of heroines who helped to change the perception of women in action-adventure movies and TV series. And she did so in great style — astride a purring, purple dream machine.

THE BATGIRL MOTORBIKE WAS THE EQUAL OF THE BATCYCLE IN EVERY WAY. THIS CUSTOMIZED STREET BIKE RAN RINGS AROUND GOTHAM CITY'S CRIMINAL UNDERCLASS, AND WAS BATGIRL'S PRIMARY MODE OF TRANSPORT.

Bulletproof windshield

Mirror with bat motif

Halogen headlight with ultraviolet night mode

First-aid kit

Make-up kit

Adjustable dual shocks

Drum brakes

Puncture-resistant tires

Twin turbo engine

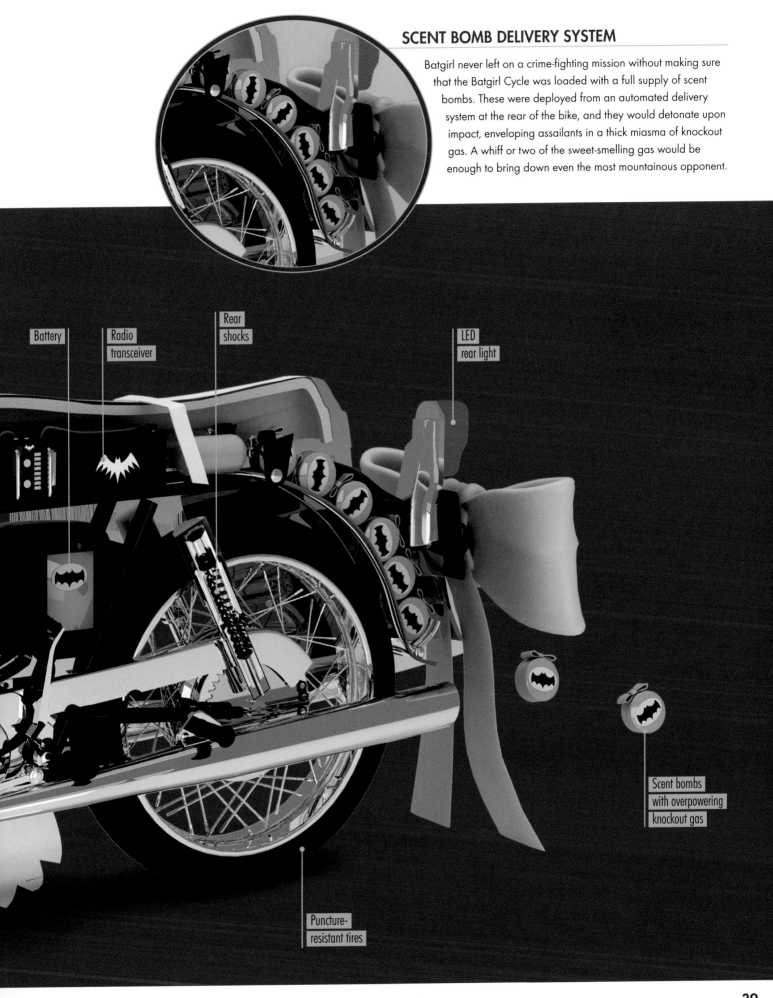

SCENT BOMB DELIVERY SYSTEM

Batgirl never left on a crime-fighting mission without making sure that the Batgirl Cycle was loaded with a full supply of scent bombs. These were deployed from an automated delivery system at the rear of the bike, and they would detonate upon impact, enveloping assailants in a thick miasma of knockout gas. A whiff or two of the sweet-smelling gas would be enough to bring down even the most mountainous opponent.

Battery

Radio transceiver

Rear shocks

LED rear light

Scent bombs with overpowering knockout gas

Puncture-resistant tires

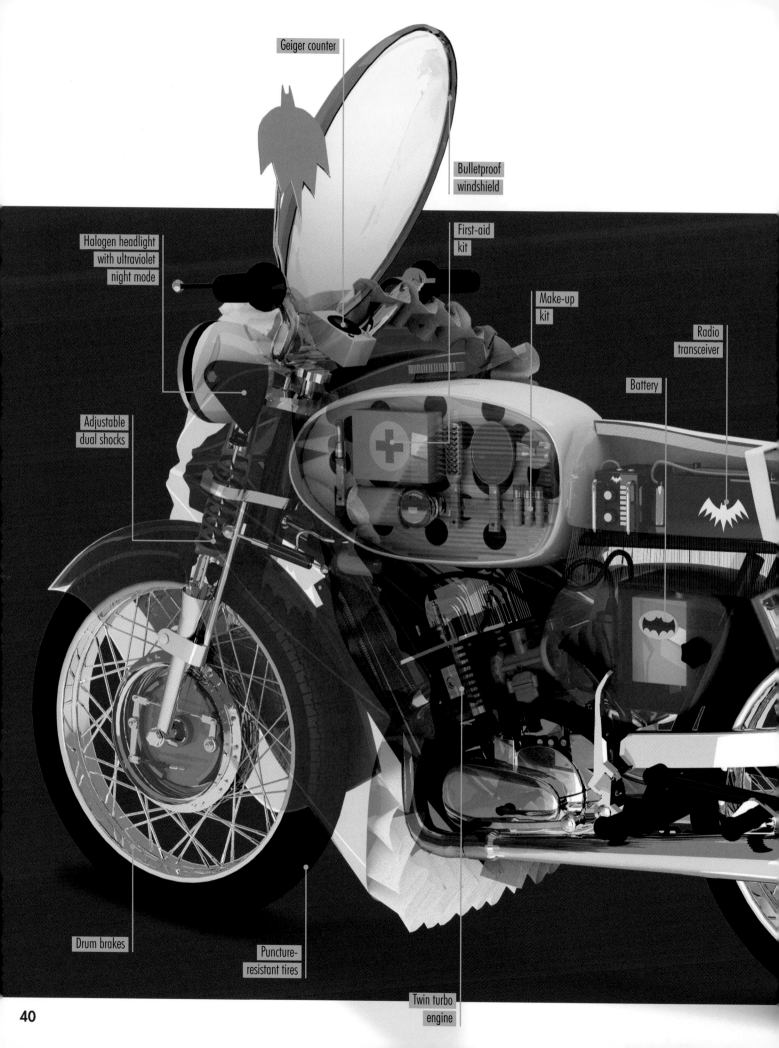

Geiger counter

Bulletproof
windshield

Halogen headlight
with ultraviolet
night mode

First-aid
kit

Make-up
kit

Radio
transceiver

Battery

Adjustable
dual shocks

Drum brakes

Puncture-
resistant tires

Twin turbo
engine

40

FIRST AID

The Batgirl Cycle was fitted with a first-aid kit that, despite its small size, contained everything Batgirl needed in case of a medical emergency. Next to this was a full make-up kit, carried not for reasons of vanity, but to ensure that Batgirl could check that her identity-concealing mask and make-up was always in perfect order.

Hidden camera

Scent bomb delivery system

SPECIFICATIONS

LENGTH 80.70 IN (2.05 M)
WIDTH 37.40 IN (0.95 M)
HEIGHT 55.11 IN (1.40 M)
WHEELBASE 51.56 IN (1.31 M)
WHEEL DIAMETER 24.40 IN (0.62 M)

SPECIAL FEATURES

WINDSHIELD AERODYNAMICALLY DESIGNED AND MADE FROM TOUGHENED THERMOPLASTIC SO AS TO BE BULLETPROOF

RADIO TRANSCEIVER TO ALLOW BATGIRL TO CALL FOR ASSISTANCE OR HACK INTO THE BAT-PHONE

HALOGEN HEADLIGHT TO PIERCE THE GLOOM AND STARTLE FELONS TRYING TO MAKE A GETAWAY

SCENT BOMBS BOMBS DETONATE TO OVERPOWER ENEMIES WITH A CLOYING KNOCKOUT GAS

MEDICAL KIT FOR ACCIDENTS AND EMERGENCIES, AND TO AID FIRST RESPONDERS IN THEIR WORK

ENGINE POWERFUL TWIN TURBO ENGINE FITTED WITH RADIOACTIVE SPARK PLUGS

TIRES FILLED WITH A REVOLUTIONARY FOAM-LIKE MATERIAL, THE TIRES ON THE BATGIRL CYCLE ARE BULLETPROOF AND PUNCTURE-RESISTANT, ALLOWING BATGIRL TO POWER THROUGH IN THE FACE OF HEAVILY ARMED OPPONENTS

ARMOR THE FRONT FAIRING IS ARMORED TO PROTECT BOTH THE RIDER AND THE BIKE'S VITAL COMPONENTS

CLOWN PRINCE OF
CARS

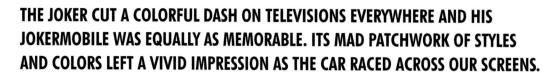

THE JOKER CUT A COLORFUL DASH ON TELEVISIONS EVERYWHERE AND HIS JOKERMOBILE WAS EQUALLY AS MEMORABLE. ITS MAD PATCHWORK OF STYLES AND COLORS LEFT A VIVID IMPRESSION AS THE CAR RACED ACROSS OUR SCREENS.

To celebrate the enduring appeal of the classic Batman TV series, DC Comics launched Batman '66 in 2013, a digital-first title that was later compiled as monthly print editions. Batman '66 #11 (July 2014) featured a team-up between the Joker and Catwoman, the crooked cohorts breaking out of the Arkham Institute for the Criminally Insane to spread madness throughout Gotham City. The villains took a Brain Regulator with them, helped in their endeavour by the naïve Doctor Holly Quinn. The psychiatrist had merely wanted to see the experimental device perfected, and she was therefore shocked when the Joker hooked it up to his Jokermobile. Energised by the Clown Prince of Crime's demented mind, the Brain Regulator transmitted waves of insanity across the city. Speeding around in the Jokermobile, the Joker spread his unique brand of lunacy – while Catwoman took advantage of the chaos to pick pockets and amass a fortune in stolen jewellery. In the end, while the Dynamic Duo and Batgirl were harassed by laughing lunatics, Holly Quinn saved the day. She hijacked the Jokermobile and used her own calm mental energies to restore normalcy. There was a cost, however, and feedback transformed the demure doctor into a new villain – the hysterical Harlequin.

TV APPEARANCES

The Jokermobile made appearances in both the second and third seasons of the classic Batman TV series. The car made its debut in "The Joker's Last Laugh" – the initial instalment of a two-parter that saw the Joker establishing a counterfeiting ring under the guise of a comic book publishing house. He laundered his funny money through the Gotham City Bank, controlling the flow of false currency through a robotic teller called Mr. Glee. Of course, Batman swiftly figured out the scam and shut down Mr. Glee, loading the android's inert form into the Batmobile. This was all part of the Joker's scheme, however, and the villain was able to track his mechanical stooge's radio emissions. Racing along in the Jokermobile, the villain chased after Batman and Robin, hoping to discover the secret location of the Batcave. The Caped Crusader was wise to the villain's plot, though, and led him on a merry chase to an innocuous field.

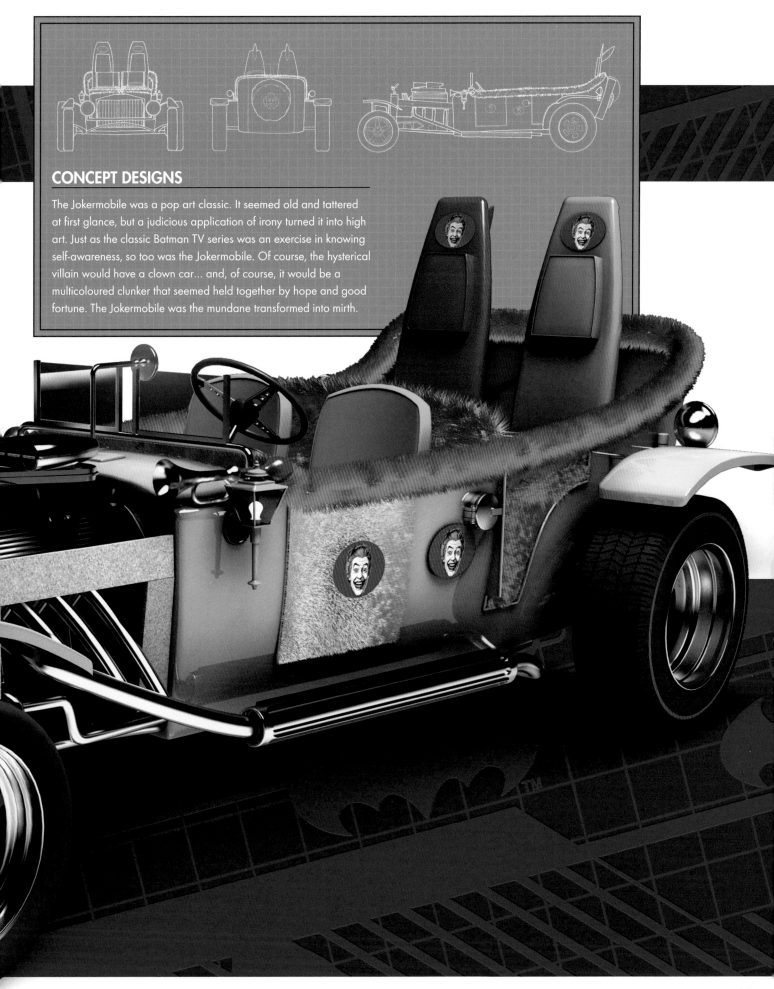

CONCEPT DESIGNS

The Jokermobile was a pop art classic. It seemed old and tattered at first glance, but a judicious application of irony turned it into high art. Just as the classic Batman TV series was an exercise in knowing self-awareness, so too was the Jokermobile. Of course, the hysterical villain would have a clown car... and, of course, it would be a multicoloured clunker that seemed held together by hope and good fortune. The Jokermobile was the mundane transformed into mirth.

THE JOKERMOBILE WAS A GLORIOUSLY GAUDY VEHICLE THAT CAPTURED PERFECTLY THE LUNATIC VILLAIN'S QUIXOTIC NATURE. WITH COUNTLESS TRICKS AND A LUXURIOUS FUR-LINED INTERIOR, THIS WAS THE CROWN PRINCE OF CLOWN CARS.

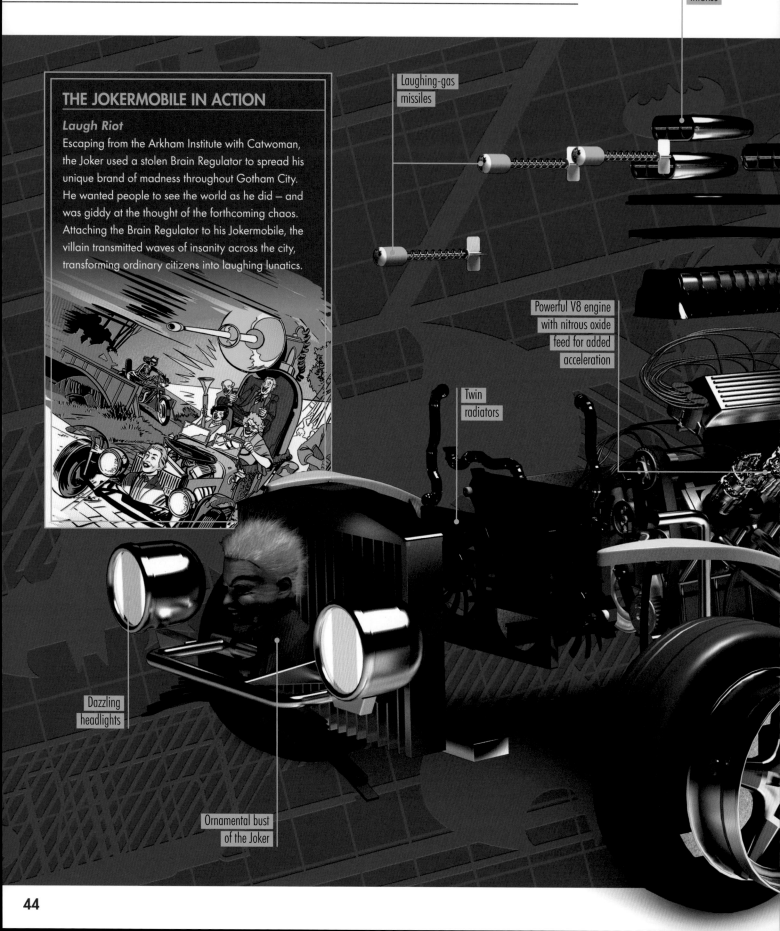

Engine supercharger intakes

Laughing-gas missiles

THE JOKERMOBILE IN ACTION

Laugh Riot

Escaping from the Arkham Institute with Catwoman, the Joker used a stolen Brain Regulator to spread his unique brand of madness throughout Gotham City. He wanted people to see the world as he did — and was giddy at the thought of the forthcoming chaos. Attaching the Brain Regulator to his Jokermobile, the villain transmitted waves of insanity across the city, transforming ordinary citizens into laughing lunatics.

Powerful V8 engine with nitrous oxide feed for added acceleration

Twin radiators

Dazzling headlights

Ornamental bust of the Joker

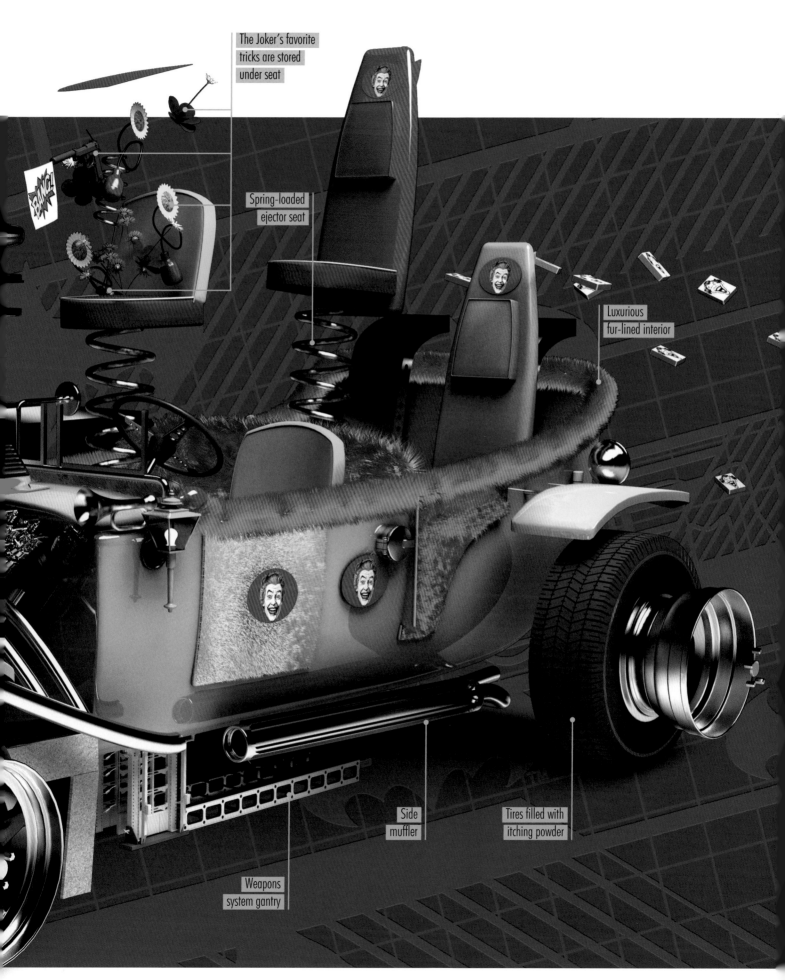

The Joker's favorite tricks are stored under seat

Spring-loaded ejector seat

Luxurious fur-lined interior

Weapons system gantry

Side muffler

Tires filled with itching powder

SPECIFICATIONS

HEIGHT 67.32 IN (1.71 M)
LENGTH 162.99 IN (4.14 M)
WIDTH 81.89 IN (2.08 M)
WHEELBASE 120.08 IN (3.05 M)

SPECIAL FEATURES

DECORATIVE BUST A BUST OF THE JOKER SERVES TO FUEL THE VILLAIN'S IMMENSE EGO, BUT ALSO DOUBLES AS A POWERFUL WATER CANNON

TRICKS OF THE TRADE THE JOKER'S CRIMINAL TRICKS, SUCH AS JOY BUZZERS AND GAS-SQUIRTING FLOWERS, ARE STORED IN A COMPARTMENT BENEATH THE DRIVING SEAT

LAUGHING-GAS MISSILES TO INCAPACITATE THE POLICE OR ANYONE ELSE IN HOT PURSUIT OF THE JOKER AND HIS GOONS

EJECTOR SEATS SPRING-LOADED EJECTOR SEATS ADD COMEDY FLAIR TO THE JOKER'S GETAWAYS

LUXURIOUS INTERIOR ONLY THE BEST IS GOOD ENOUGH FOR THE CLOWN PRINCE OF CRIME AND HIS FELLOW VILLAINS

SLASH-RESISTANT TIRES IN ADDITION TO BEING BULLETPROOF AND SLASH-RESISTANT, THE CAR'S TIRES ARE ALSO FILLED WITH ITCHING POWDER

DAZZLING HEADLIGHTS DESIGNED TO CAUSE TEMPORARY BLINDNESS SO THAT THE JOKER AND HIS HENCHMEN CAN GO ABOUT THEIR CROOKED BUSINESS WITHOUT INTERFERENCE

Engine supercharger intakes

BANG!

Engine supercharger

Dazzling headlights

Twin radiators

Powerful V8 engine with nitrous oxide feed for added acceleration

Weapons system gantry

The Joker's favorite tricks are stored under seat

Spring-loaded ejector seats

Packs of exploding playing cards dispersed from rear

Luxurious fur-lined interior

Spare tire

Tires filled with itching powder

PREDATOR WHEELS

CATWOMAN STALKED THE STREETS OF GOTHAM CITY IN A RIDE THAT WAS AS OSTENTATIOUS AS THE VILLAIN HERSELF. NICKNAMED THE KITTY CAR, THIS BIZARRE VEHICLE WAS A MOTORIZED PREDATOR ON THE PROWL FOR PLUNDER.

Catwoman can't be accused of slumming it. She had a taste for the finer things in life and her first criminal car reflected a seemingly unquenchable thirst for opulence. The luxurious "Catillac" was featured in the second season of the classic Batman TV series, used by the villain as a getaway car to escape the pursuing Batmobile.

As the villain's crooked schemes grew more ambitious, the Catillac was replaced by the outrageous Kitty Car — which made its debut in the third season episode, "Funny Feline Felonies."

While the Kitty Car was every bit as extravagant as her previous set of wheels – with faux leather interiors, for instance – it was anything but a regular ride. Rather, it was a concept car customized to aid Catwoman in her criminal endeavors. Like a sleek and sinuous predator, the Kitty Car's claws were kept out of sight until needed. When Catwoman sped into action, however, she unleashed the Kitty Car's numerous weapons – a buzz-saw, stingers and even a whipping tail.

CATWOMAN IN ACTION!

Catwoman also starred in the bestselling Batman '66 comic book. She's helped spring the Joker from the Arkham Institute, played cat-and-mouse games with Batgirl and even opened a nightclub. In Batman '66 #29 (January 2016), she helped Batman to save Robin and Batgirl from a host of deadly super-villains. Leaping into the Batmobile she cried playfully, "Atomic batteries to whatever, turbines to bee-bop!"

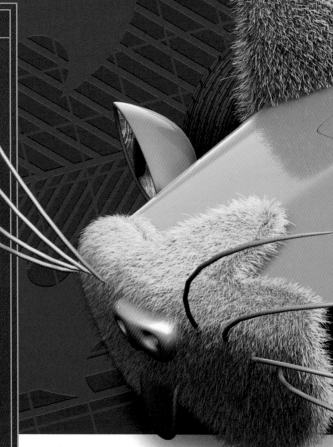

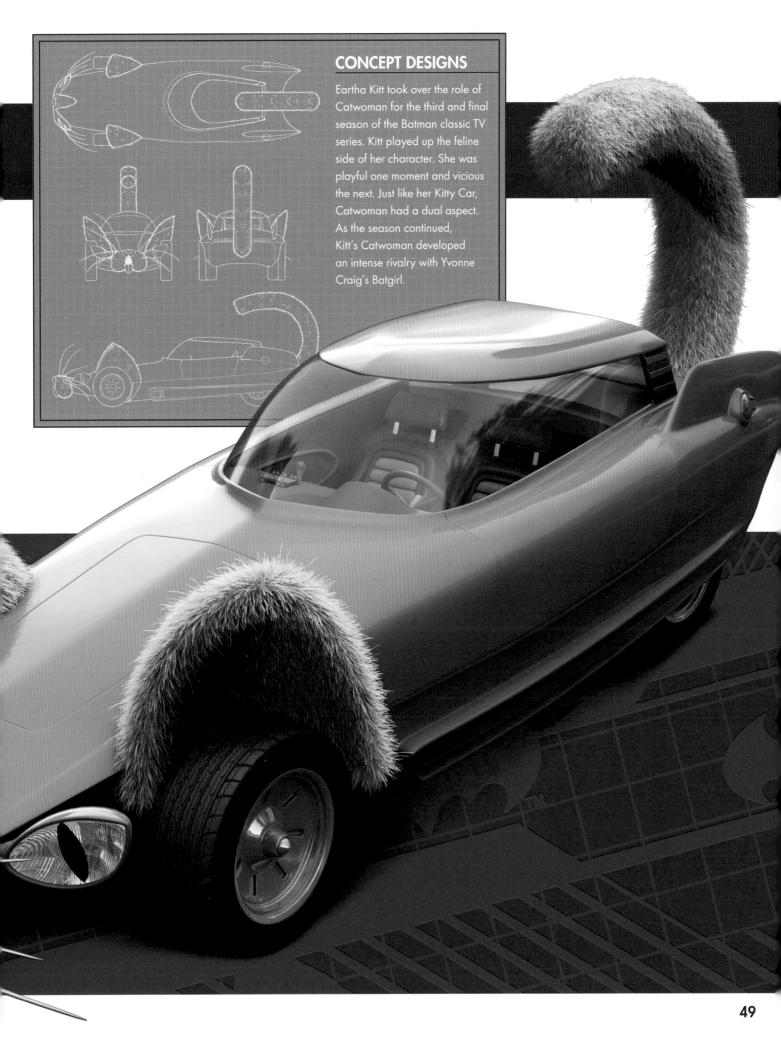

CONCEPT DESIGNS

Eartha Kitt took over the role of Catwoman for the third and final season of the Batman classic TV series. Kitt played up the feline side of her character. She was playful one moment and vicious the next. Just like her Kitty Car, Catwoman had a dual aspect. As the season continued, Kitt's Catwoman developed an intense rivalry with Yvonne Craig's Batgirl.

THE KITTY CAR HAD THE BEST OF EVERYTHING. IT WAS
A LUXURIOUS RIDE WITH SUMPTUOUS UPHOLSTERY AND A
POWERFUL SPORTS-CAR ENGINE. LIKE ITS OWNER, THE KITTY
CAR WAS SLEEK AND SINUOUS — BUT IT WAS ALSO DEADLY.

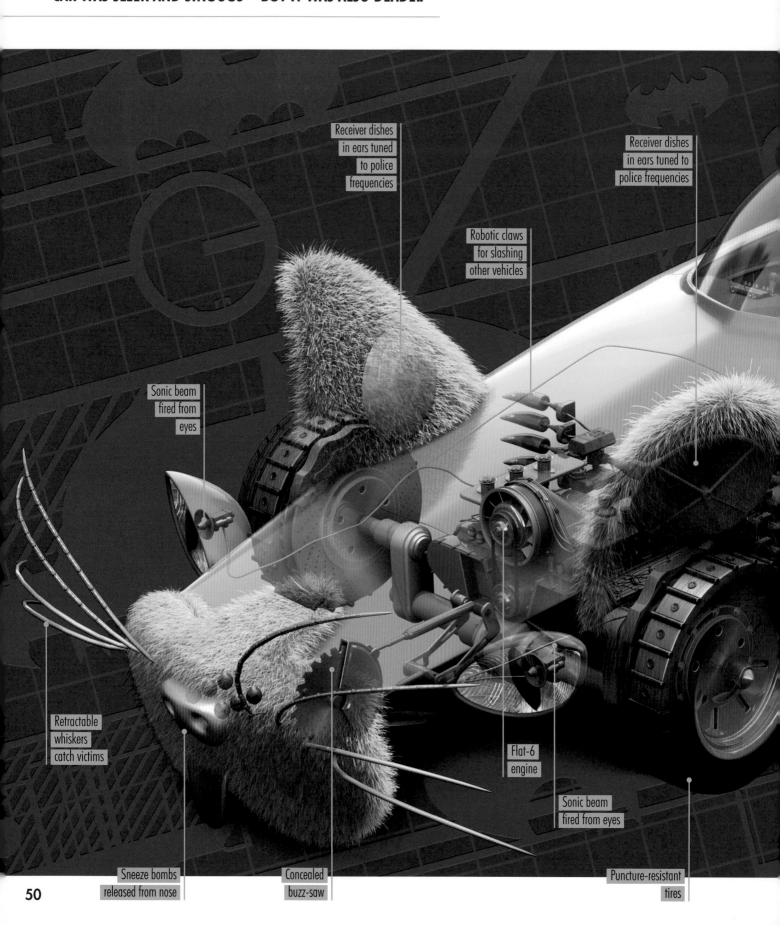

Receiver dishes
in ears tuned
to police
frequencies

Receiver dishes
in ears tuned to
police frequencies

Robotic claws
for slashing
other vehicles

Sonic beam
fired from
eyes

Retractable
whiskers
catch victims

Flat-6
engine

Sonic beam
fired from eyes

Sneeze bombs
released from nose

Concealed
buzz-saw

Puncture-resistant
tires

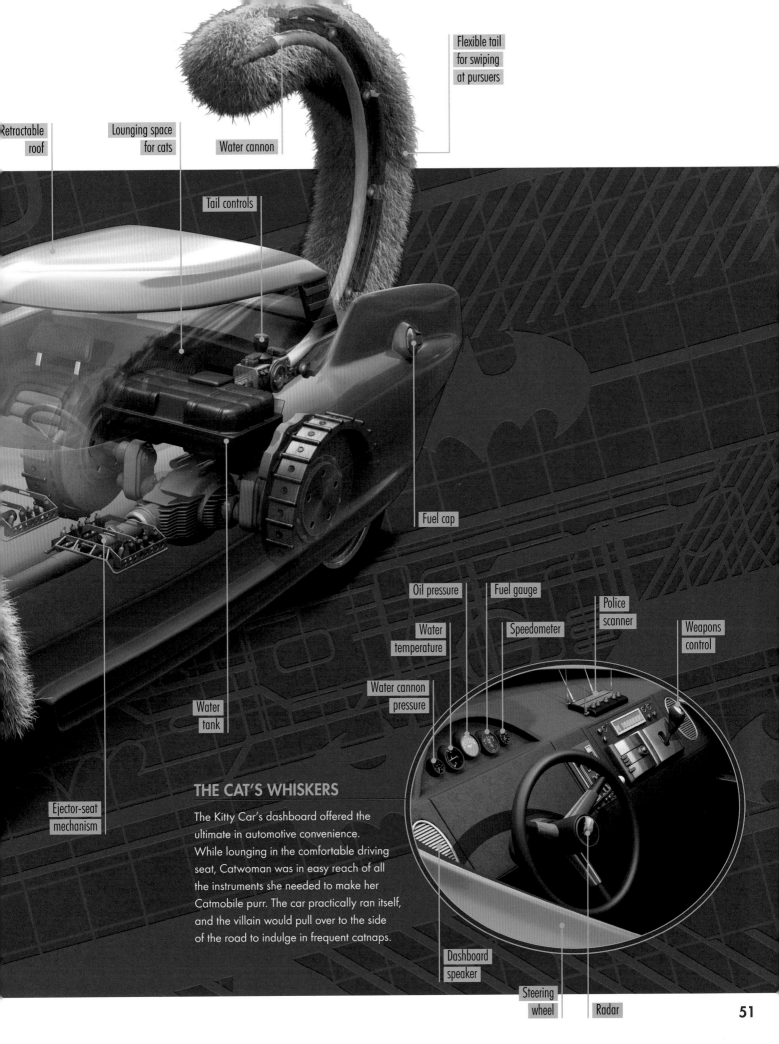

Flexible tail
for swiping
at pursuers

Retractable
roof

Lounging space
for cats

Water cannon

Tail controls

Fuel cap

Oil pressure

Fuel gauge

Water
temperature

Speedometer

Police
scanner

Weapons
control

Water cannon
pressure

Water
tank

Ejector-seat
mechanism

THE CAT'S WHISKERS

The Kitty Car's dashboard offered the
ultimate in automotive convenience.
While lounging in the comfortable driving
seat, Catwoman was in easy reach of all
the instruments she needed to make her
Catmobile purr. The car practically ran itself,
and the villain would pull over to the side
of the road to indulge in frequent catnaps.

Dashboard
speaker

Steering
wheel

Radar

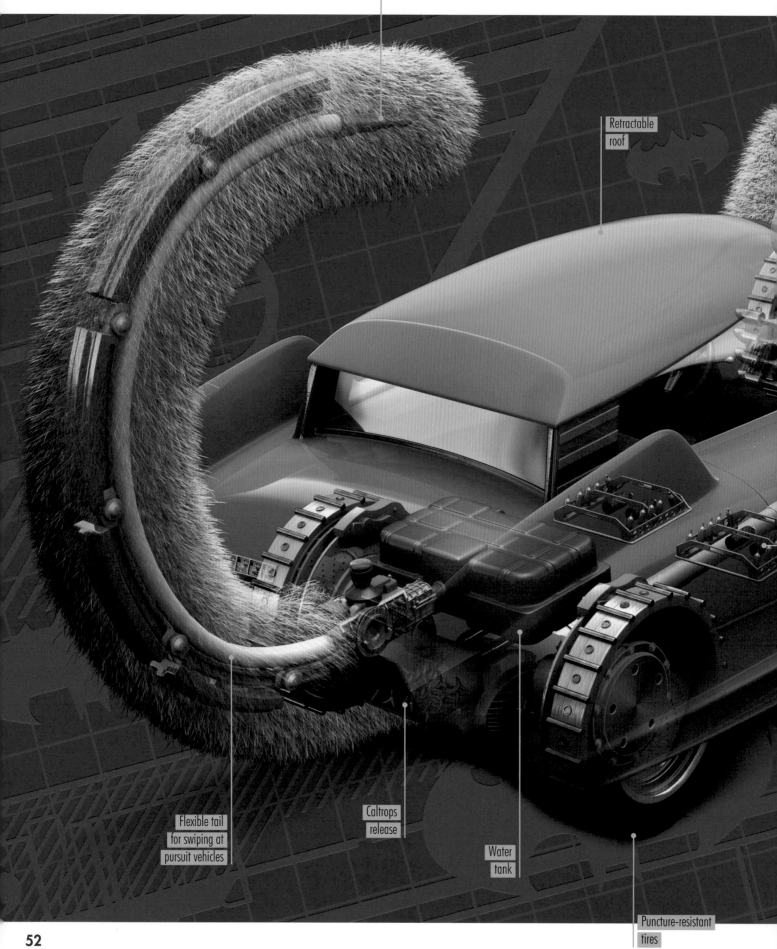

Water
cannon

Retractable
roof

Flexible tail
for swiping at
pursuit vehicles

Caltrops
release

Water
tank

Puncture-resistant
tires

Retractable whiskers catch victims

Tire slasher

Ejector-seat mechanism

SPECIFICATIONS

LENGTH 250.00 IN (6.35 M)
HEIGHT (WITH TAIL) 96.85 IN (2.46 M)
WIDTH 88.98 IN (2.26 M)
WHEELBASE 130.31 IN (3.31 M)

SPECIAL FEATURES

CRUSHING TAIL WHIPS DOWN AT TREMENDOUS SPEED TO SMASH THE BONNETS OF PURSUING VEHICLES

BUZZ-SAW THE CAT FACE FLIPS UP TO REVEAL A WHIRRING BUZZ-SAW CAPABLE OF SLICING THROUGH MOST OBSTACLES

SONIC BEAM A CONCENTRATED SOUND WAVE IS EMITTED FROM THE CAR'S EYES TO INCAPACITATE VICTIMS AND DESTROY OBJECTS

ROBOTIC CLAWS HYDRAULIC CLAWS EMERGE FROM THE SIDES OF THE KITTY CAR TO SLASH AT RIVAL VEHICLES

HYPERSENSITIVE WHISKERS RESPONDING TO BODY HEAT, THESE TELESCOPIC FILAMENTS SNAKE OUT TO CATCH VICTIMS AND ARE ALSO USED AS A DEADLY CAT-O'-NINE-TAILS

LOUNGING AREA THE KITTY CAR HAS NO REAR PASSENGER SEATS. INSTEAD, THE AREA IS RESERVED AS A RELAXATION SPACE FOR CATWOMAN'S MANY FELINE FRIENDS

EARS RADIO TRANSCEIVERS WITHIN THE CAR'S CAT-LIKE EARS ALLOW CATWOMAN TO LISTEN TO POLICE BROADCASTS, AS WELL AS TRANSMIT INSTRUCTIONS TO HER HENCHMEN

SNEEZE BOMBS FIRED FROM THE KITTY CAR'S NOSE, THE SNEEZE BOMBS PRODUCE A CHOKING MIASMA ON DETONATION

WATER CANNON THE KITTY CAR'S TAIL ALSO DOUBLES AS A POWERFUL WATER CANNON

THE WIDOW'S BIKE

AT FIRST GLANCE, THE BLACK WIDOW LOOKED LIKE A DEMURE, HARMLESS OLD LADY. ARMED WITH A "CEREBRUM SHORT-CIRCUITOR" AND A CUSTOMIZED MOTORCYCLE, HOWEVER, THIS POISONOUS CREATURE PROVED TO BE ANYTHING BUT!

The Black Widow traveled around Gotham City in style, cruising from bank to bank in the side-car of a motorcycle steered by one of her minions. Using a gadget of her own devising, she scrambled the brains of bank managers – persuading them to open up their vaults, before speeding back to her underground lair.

But the Black Widow hadn't factored in the tenaciousness of the Dynamic Duo. Figuring out that the ingenious villain was hitting Gotham City's banks in alphabetical order, Batman and Robin followed her to her hideaway, before swiftly bringing her to justice.

The Black Widow was revived in the Batman '66 comic book. Teaming up with the Penguin in #15 (November 2014), she unleashed a crime wave on Gotham City. Commanding a giant man-eating spider called Lulah, she wanted revenge on all men. But once Batman persuaded the Penguin that his new partner couldn't be trusted, the waddling villain switched sides. In the ensuing confrontation, the Black Widow fell through Lulah's web and was taken to jail.

THE BLACK WIDOW IN ACTION

HEY! THE WHOLE WEB! IT'S STARTING TO COME...

...DOWN!

IT'S THE CUMULATIVE EFFECT OF THE PENGUIN'S SPRAY!

GRAB HOLD OF SOMETHING!

A-AAH!!

NO, YOU CAN'T HAVE—

AAAAHH!!

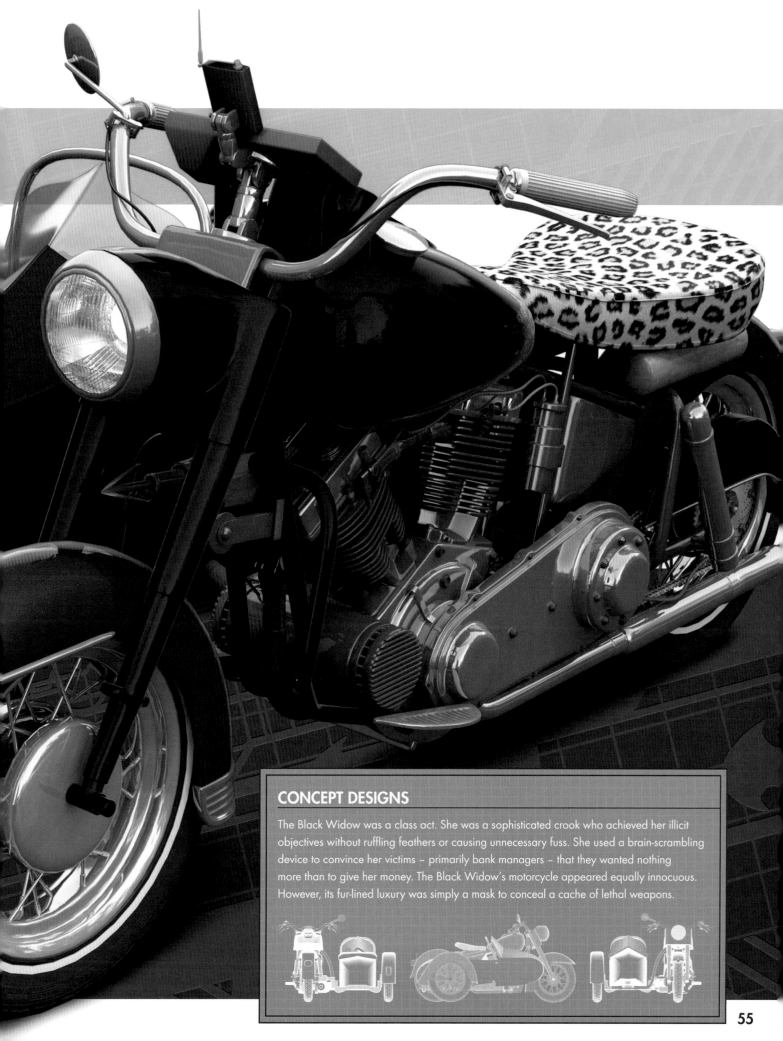

CONCEPT DESIGNS

The Black Widow was a class act. She was a sophisticated crook who achieved her illicit objectives without ruffling feathers or causing unnecessary fuss. She used a brain-scrambling device to convince her victims – primarily bank managers – that they wanted nothing more than to give her money. The Black Widow's motorcycle appeared equally innocuous. However, its fur-lined luxury was simply a mask to conceal a cache of lethal weapons.

THE BLACK WIDOW RODE THE SIDECAR OF HER MOTORCYCLE LIKE A CHARIOTEER OF OLD. FITTED WITH WEAPONS TO BAFFLE AND PARALYZE HER VICTIMS, THE BIKE WAS A DEADLY INSTRUMENT IN THE BLACK WIDOW'S CAMPAIGN OF EVIL.

Side mirror

Headlight with strobing effects

Venom dispenser

Black Widow symbol

Sidecar's front wheel

Grappling hook

Panhead engine

Mudguard

Gel-filled tires

Front fork

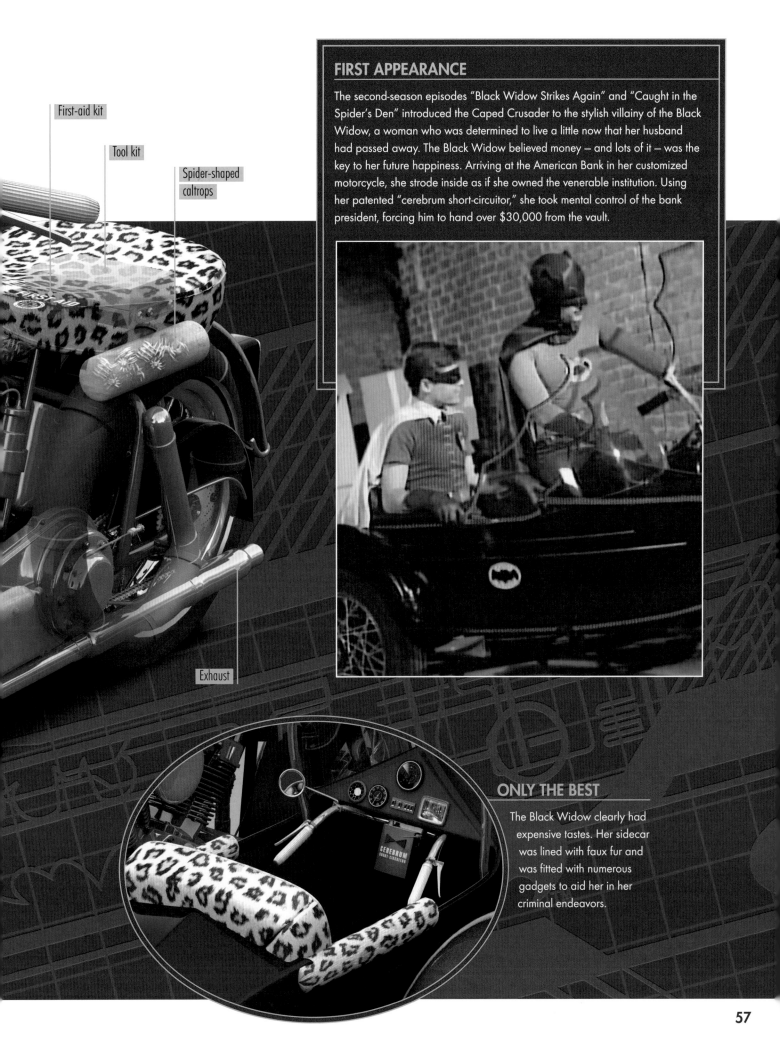

First-aid kit

Tool kit

Spider-shaped caltrops

Exhaust

FIRST APPEARANCE

The second-season episodes "Black Widow Strikes Again" and "Caught in the Spider's Den" introduced the Caped Crusader to the stylish villainy of the Black Widow, a woman who was determined to live a little now that her husband had passed away. The Black Widow believed money — and lots of it — was the key to her future happiness. Arriving at the American Bank in her customized motorcycle, she strode inside as if she owned the venerable institution. Using her patented "cerebrum short-circuitor," she took mental control of the bank president, forcing him to hand over $30,000 from the vault.

ONLY THE BEST

The Black Widow clearly had expensive tastes. Her sidecar was lined with faux fur and was fitted with numerous gadgets to aid her in her criminal endeavors.

Leopard
print seat
cover

First-aid
kit

Tool kit

Spider-shaped
caltrops

Rear tail light

SPECIFICATIONS

LENGTH 83.86 IN (2.13 M)
WIDTH (WITH SIDECAR) 60.63 IN (1.54 M)
HEIGHT 53.54 IN (1.36 M)
WHEELBASE 57.87 IN (1.47 M)

SPECIAL FEATURES

PARALYZING VENOM A FAST-ACTING NERVE TOXIN IS SHOT FROM THE
MOTORCYCLE'S SIDECAR TO RENDER THE BLACK WIDOW'S PREY IMMOBILE

BLINDING HEADLIGHT WITH A STROBING EFFECT TO DISORIENTATE
POTENTIAL WITNESSES AND DETER PURSUIT

SIDE-CAR FITTED WITH AN ELECTRICAL MOTOR AND INDEPENDENT
STEERING SYSTEM TO ALLOW THE BLACK WIDOW TO RACE INTO ACTION ON
HER OWN

GRAPPLING HOOK USED BY THE VILLAIN'S HENCHMEN TO SCALE THE
WALLS OF BANKS AND BULLION DEPOSITORIES

TIRES FILLED WITH A REVOLUTIONARY GEL-LIKE MATERIAL, THE BIKE'S
TIRES ARE BULLETPROOF AND PUNCTURE-RESISTANT

REINFORCED RIMS THE BIKE'S RIMS AND SPOKES ARE ULTRA-STRONG
TO COPE WITH JARRING COLLISIONS

RADIO TRANSCEIVER ENABLES BLACK WIDOW TO KEEP IN CONSTANT
COMMUNICATION WITH HER HENCHMAN SHOULD THE BIKE AND SIDECAR
BECOME SEPARATED

WEB-CANNON FIRES A STICKY FLUID OF BLACK WIDOW'S OWN
INVENTION TO TRAP VICTIMS

Gel-filled tires

Webbing
dispenser

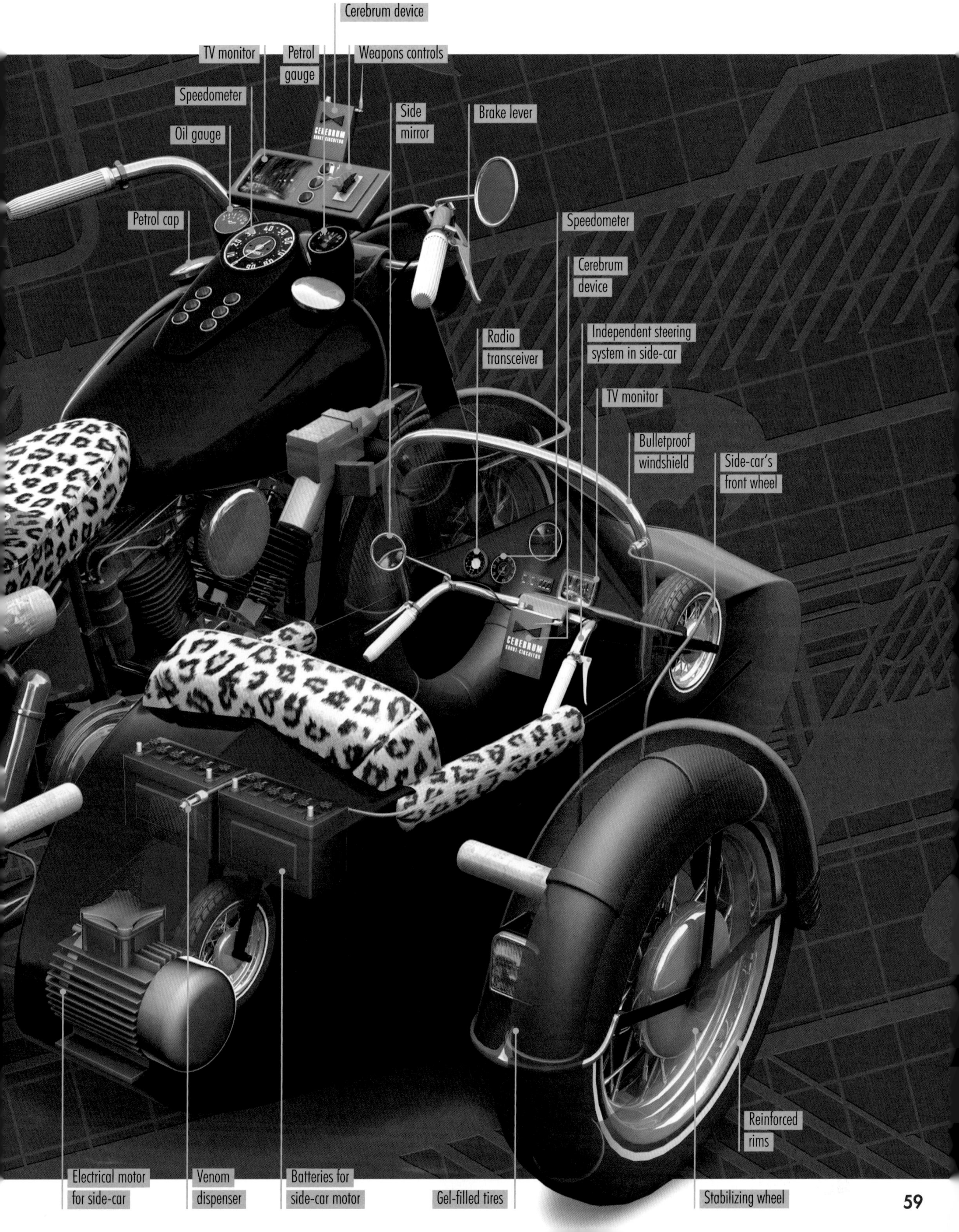

Cerebrum device

TV monitor

Petrol gauge

Weapons controls

Speedometer

Side mirror

Brake lever

Oil gauge

Petrol cap

Speedometer

Cerebrum device

Independent steering system in side-car

Radio transceiver

TV monitor

Bulletproof windshield

Side-car's front wheel

Electrical motor for side-car

Venom dispenser

Batteries for side-car motor

Gel-filled tires

Stabilizing wheel

Reinforced rims

CUCKOO IN THE NEST

THE BATMOBILE FROM THE CLASSIC BATMAN TV SERIES IS AN ICONIC CAR, AND EVEN THE PERFIDIOUS PENGUIN ADMIRED IT FROM AFAR. SO NATURALLY, WHEN THE OPPORTUNITY AROSE, HE COULDN'T RESIST SNATCHING IT FOR HIMSELF.

After absconding with the Batmobile, the crooked Penguin decided to make a few modifications to make the car more to his liking. He fitted a parasol to protect fiancée Sophia Starr from the sun's rays, and painted a new logo on the door so everyone would know that this was now the Birdmobile!

These were simple cosmetic changes, however, and nothing the Penguin could do would ever alter the true nature of the Batmobile.

The nefarious Penguin was more than familiar with the Batmobile's crime-fighting arsenal, having come face-to-face with much of

it during his villainous career. There were some gadgets, however, that the devious criminal knew nothing about. He certainly knew nothing of Batman fitting the famous car with remote-control circuitry, which he then used to control the car's ejector seats from a distance — propelling the Penguin from the Batmobile at the earliest opportunity!

CONCEPT DESIGNS

In the summer of 1965, the producers of the Batman TV show asked custom-car mechanic George Barris to build them a Batmobile. There was just one catch: the vehicle had to be finished and ready for filming in a matter of weeks. Fortunately, Barris already owned a concept car — the Lincoln Futura — that he believed had enough bat-like qualities to make it the ideal template. With modifications to the bodywork and the addition of numerous gadgets, the Batmobile was duly born. The car was a huge success, and Barris and his team went on to build three fiberglass replicas that toured car shows for many years.

THE PENGUIN ADDED AN UMBRELLA GUN AND A PENGUIN-THEMED LOGO, BUT THERE WAS STILL NO MISTAKING THE ICONIC BATMOBILE. DETERMINED TO GET HIS CAR BACK, BATMAN USED THE BATMOBILE'S REMOTE-CONTROL CIRCUITRY TO EVICT THE CUCKOO IN THE VEHICULAR NEST.

Twin turbines

Bulletproof canopy

Phone to Batcave and police HQ

Twin wishbone suspension

Rotating chain slicer and battering ram

Fuel cell backup

Fuel cells

Anti-lock disk brakes

Vented
tailgate

Parasol

Rocket
system

Fire
extinguisher

Atomic
batteries

Umbrella gun
with gas
ordnance

Self-sealing
bulletproof tires

FEATHERING HIS NEST

Pleased with his purloined prize, the
Penguin wanted the world to know
that the Batmobile was now the
Birdmobile. He added a penguin
motif to the doors — and couldn't
stop chortling to himself as he toured
the streets of Gotham City in style.

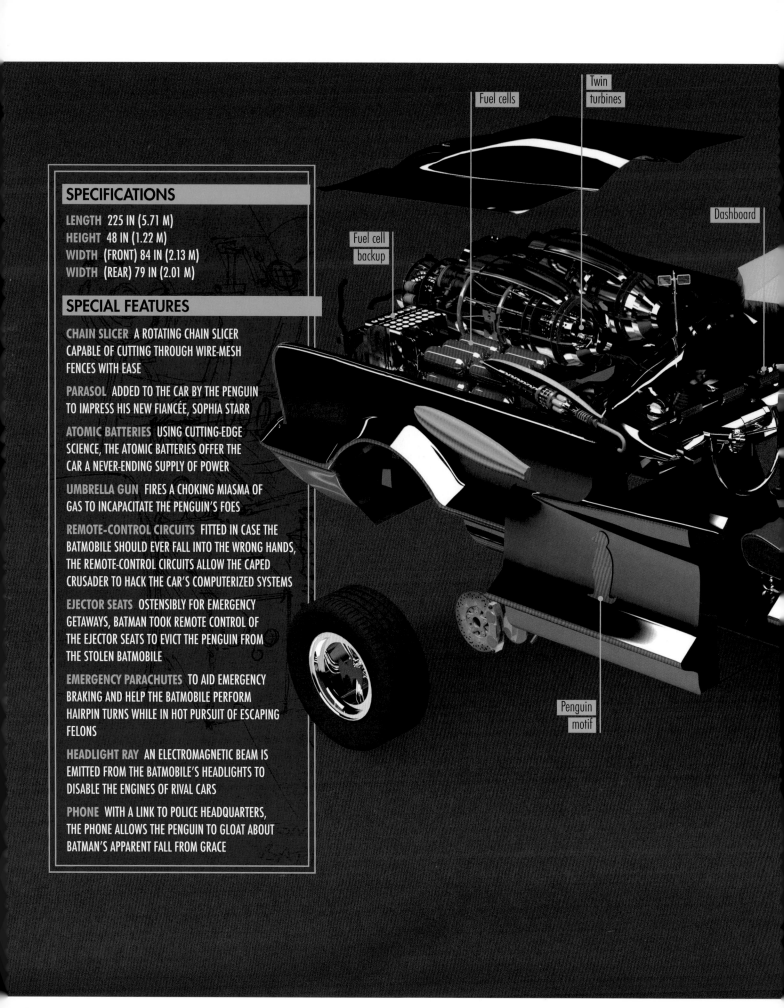

SPECIFICATIONS

LENGTH 225 IN (5.71 M)
HEIGHT 48 IN (1.22 M)
WIDTH (FRONT) 84 IN (2.13 M)
WIDTH (REAR) 79 IN (2.01 M)

SPECIAL FEATURES

CHAIN SLICER A ROTATING CHAIN SLICER
CAPABLE OF CUTTING THROUGH WIRE-MESH
FENCES WITH EASE

PARASOL ADDED TO THE CAR BY THE PENGUIN
TO IMPRESS HIS NEW FIANCÉE, SOPHIA STARR

ATOMIC BATTERIES USING CUTTING-EDGE
SCIENCE, THE ATOMIC BATTERIES OFFER THE
CAR A NEVER-ENDING SUPPLY OF POWER

UMBRELLA GUN FIRES A CHOKING MIASMA OF
GAS TO INCAPACITATE THE PENGUIN'S FOES

REMOTE-CONTROL CIRCUITS FITTED IN CASE THE
BATMOBILE SHOULD EVER FALL INTO THE WRONG HANDS,
THE REMOTE-CONTROL CIRCUITS ALLOW THE CAPED
CRUSADER TO HACK THE CAR'S COMPUTERIZED SYSTEMS

EJECTOR SEATS OSTENSIBLY FOR EMERGENCY
GETAWAYS, BATMAN TOOK REMOTE CONTROL OF
THE EJECTOR SEATS TO EVICT THE PENGUIN FROM
THE STOLEN BATMOBILE

EMERGENCY PARACHUTES TO AID EMERGENCY
BRAKING AND HELP THE BATMOBILE PERFORM
HAIRPIN TURNS WHILE IN HOT PURSUIT OF ESCAPING
FELONS

HEADLIGHT RAY AN ELECTROMAGNETIC BEAM IS
EMITTED FROM THE BATMOBILE'S HEADLIGHTS TO
DISABLE THE ENGINES OF RIVAL CARS

PHONE WITH A LINK TO POLICE HEADQUARTERS,
THE PHONE ALLOWS THE PENGUIN TO GLOAT ABOUT
BATMAN'S APPARENT FALL FROM GRACE

Fuel cells

Twin turbines

Dashboard

Fuel cell backup

Penguin motif

Parasol

Vented tailgate

Atomic batteries

Atomic batteries

Anti-lock disk brakes

Afterburner

SIMPLICITY ITSELF

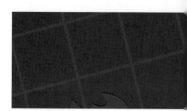

A REGULAR FEATURE OF BOTH THE ADVENTURES OF BATMAN AND THE NEW ADVENTURES OF BATMAN, THIS WAS A SLEEK AND SLENDER BATMOBILE THAT FUNCTIONED PERFECTLY IN THE PARED-DOWN WORLD OF TELEVISION ANIMATION.

Saturday-morning cartoons have been a feature of TV programming since the 1960s, and comic-book characters are a natural for the format and time-slot. Batman made his cartoon debut as part of The Batman-Superman Hour, produced by Filmation Studios for the 1968/1969 autumn season. The Caped Crusader's segments were repackaged as *The Adventures of Batman*, and for a second time as *Batman with Robin the Boy Wonder*. Naturally, the Batmobile featured heavily, with the title sequence making great play of the car — the narrator describing how the Dynamic Duo used it to "roar out to protect life, limb and property as Batman and Robin — caped crime fighters!"

Despite the budgetary limitations of TV animation, the Batmobile had many gadgets, including "hover jets" which allowed it to take to the air in pursuit of Catwoman after the feline villain shredded its tires. When Filmation returned to Batman in 1977, it reused many of the model sheets for the original show. The sleek Batmobile had a second lease of life in *The New Adventures of Batman* – captivating even more fans.

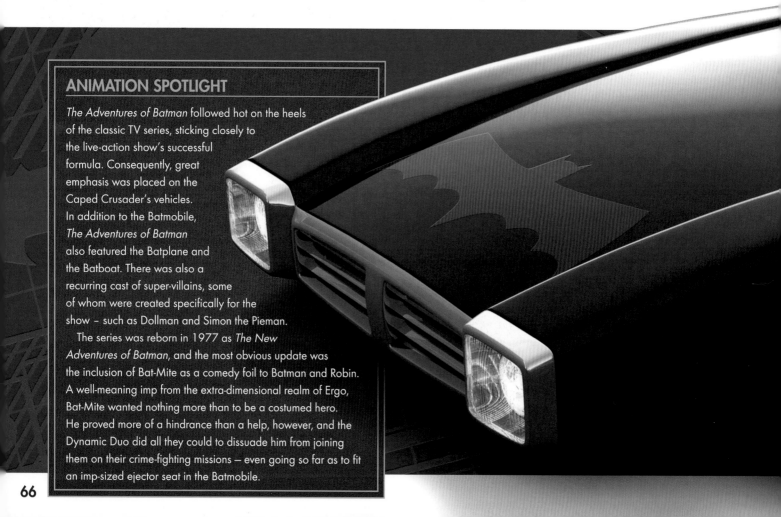

ANIMATION SPOTLIGHT

The Adventures of Batman followed hot on the heels of the classic TV series, sticking closely to the live-action show's successful formula. Consequently, great emphasis was placed on the Caped Crusader's vehicles. In addition to the Batmobile, *The Adventures of Batman* also featured the Batplane and the Batboat. There was also a recurring cast of super-villains, some of whom were created specifically for the show – such as Dollman and Simon the Pieman.

The series was reborn in 1977 as *The New Adventures of Batman*, and the most obvious update was the inclusion of Bat-Mite as a comedy foil to Batman and Robin. A well-meaning imp from the extra-dimensional realm of Ergo, Bat-Mite wanted nothing more than to be a costumed hero. He proved more of a hindrance than a help, however, and the Dynamic Duo did all they could to dissuade him from joining them on their crime-fighting missions — even going so far as to fit an imp-sized ejector seat in the Batmobile.

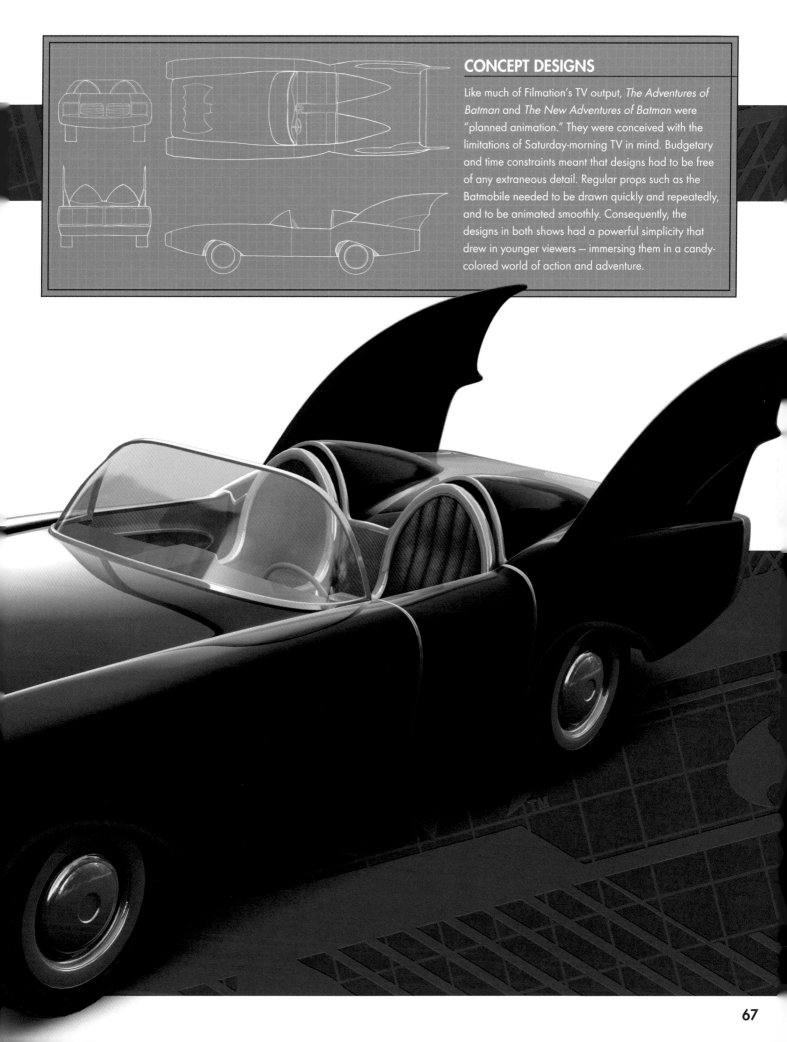

CONCEPT DESIGNS

Like much of Filmation's TV output, *The Adventures of Batman* and *The New Adventures of Batman* were "planned animation." They were conceived with the limitations of Saturday-morning TV in mind. Budgetary and time constraints meant that designs had to be free of any extraneous detail. Regular props such as the Batmobile needed to be drawn quickly and repeatedly, and to be animated smoothly. Consequently, the designs in both shows had a powerful simplicity that drew in younger viewers — immersing them in a candy-colored world of action and adventure.

THIS WAS A BATMOBILE ALL ABOUT SHAPE AND FORM. IT WAS A VEHICULAR DART THAT SHOT THROUGH THE CONCRETE CANYONS OF GOTHAM CITY WITHOUT HINDRANCE. HIDDEN WITHIN THE CAR, HOWEVER, WERE CUSTOM EXTRAS THAT OFTEN DEFIED THE IMAGINATION.

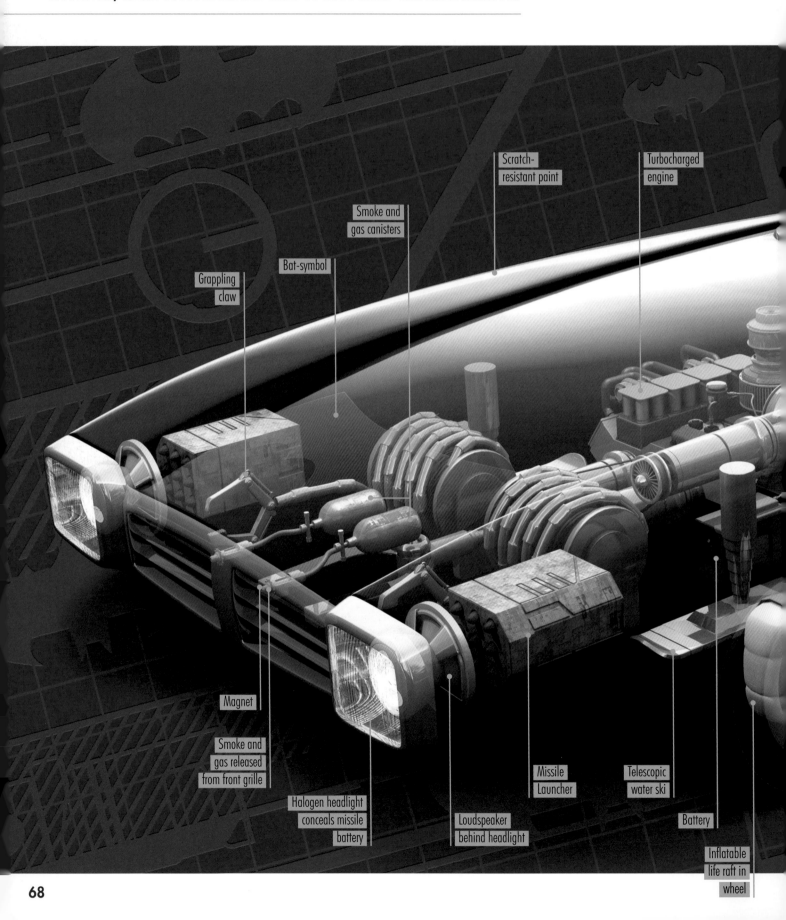

Scratch-resistant paint

Turbocharged engine

Smoke and gas canisters

Bat-symbol

Grappling claw

Magnet

Smoke and gas released from front grille

Halogen headlight conceals missile battery

Loudspeaker behind headlight

Missile Launcher

Telescopic water ski

Battery

Inflatable life raft in wheel

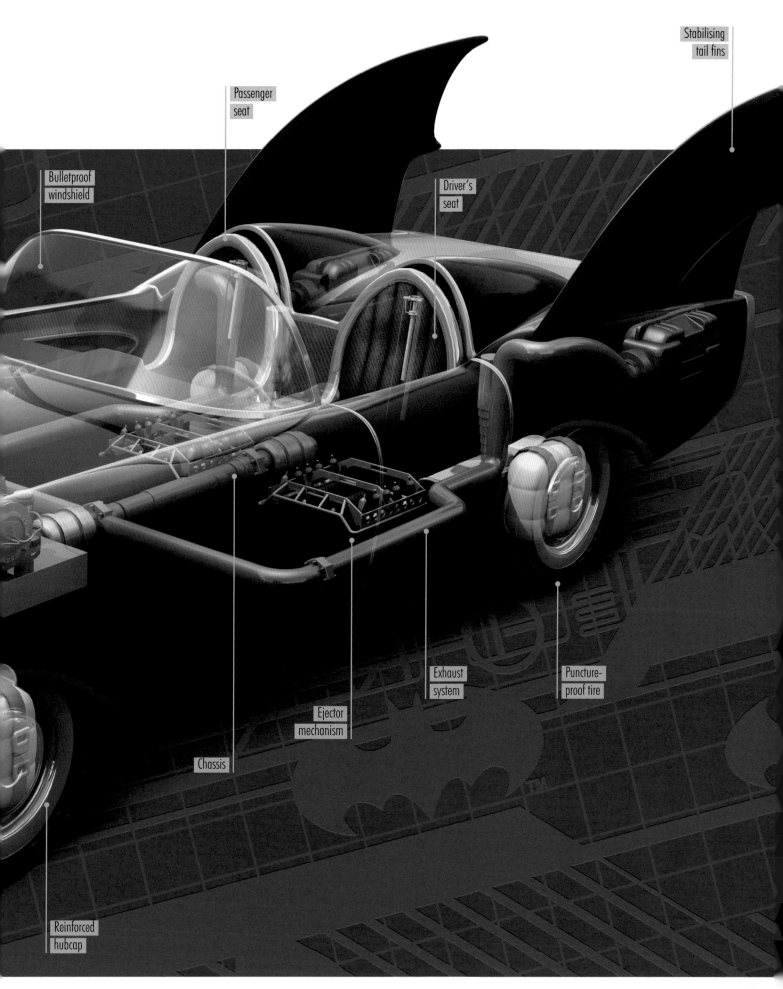

Stabilising
tail fins

Passenger
seat

Driver's
seat

Bulletproof
windshield

Exhaust
system

Puncture-
proof tire

Ejector
mechanism

Chassis

Reinforced
hubcap

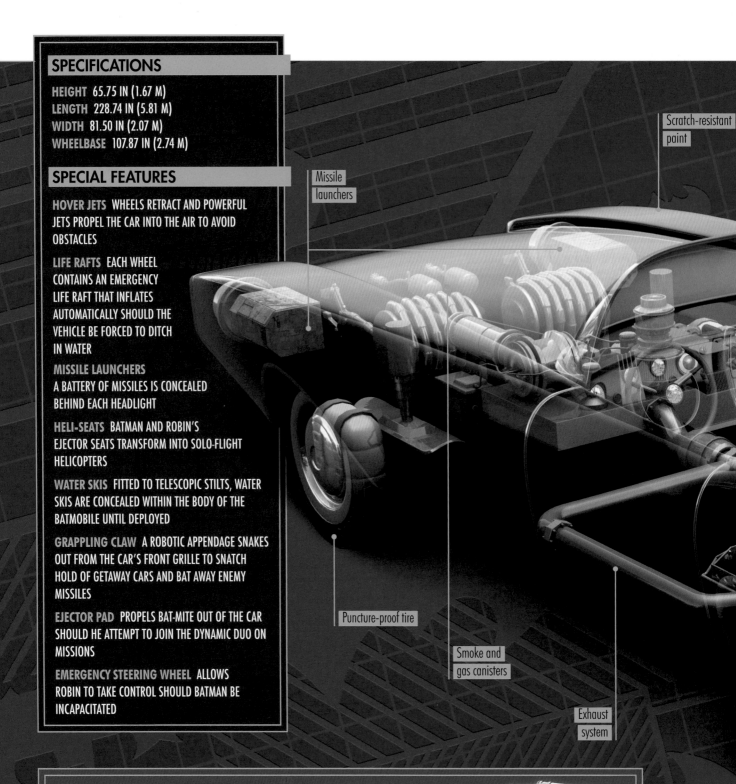

SPECIFICATIONS

HEIGHT 65.75 IN (1.67 M)
LENGTH 228.74 IN (5.81 M)
WIDTH 81.50 IN (2.07 M)
WHEELBASE 107.87 IN (2.74 M)

SPECIAL FEATURES

HOVER JETS WHEELS RETRACT AND POWERFUL JETS PROPEL THE CAR INTO THE AIR TO AVOID OBSTACLES

LIFE RAFTS EACH WHEEL CONTAINS AN EMERGENCY LIFE RAFT THAT INFLATES AUTOMATICALLY SHOULD THE VEHICLE BE FORCED TO DITCH IN WATER

MISSILE LAUNCHERS A BATTERY OF MISSILES IS CONCEALED BEHIND EACH HEADLIGHT

HELI-SEATS BATMAN AND ROBIN'S EJECTOR SEATS TRANSFORM INTO SOLO-FLIGHT HELICOPTERS

WATER SKIS FITTED TO TELESCOPIC STILTS, WATER SKIS ARE CONCEALED WITHIN THE BODY OF THE BATMOBILE UNTIL DEPLOYED

GRAPPLING CLAW A ROBOTIC APPENDAGE SNAKES OUT FROM THE CAR'S FRONT GRILLE TO SNATCH HOLD OF GETAWAY CARS AND BAT AWAY ENEMY MISSILES

EJECTOR PAD PROPELS BAT-MITE OUT OF THE CAR SHOULD HE ATTEMPT TO JOIN THE DYNAMIC DUO ON MISSIONS

EMERGENCY STEERING WHEEL ALLOWS ROBIN TO TAKE CONTROL SHOULD BATMAN BE INCAPACITATED

Scratch-resistant paint

Missile launchers

Puncture-proof tire

Smoke and gas canisters

Exhaust system

THE BATMOBILE IN ACTION

Auto acrobatics

This was a Batmobile that got the Dynamic Duo to wherever they wanted to go, even if their destination was the top of a tower block or halfway up a mountain. The car was fitted with "heli-seats" that Batman and Robin used to soar into the sky. An automated trampoline also meant that the heroes could spring up the side of buildings. The trampoline proved a useful deterrent to Bat-Mite — preventing the mischievous imp from returning to the Batmobile after he'd been ejected from the car.

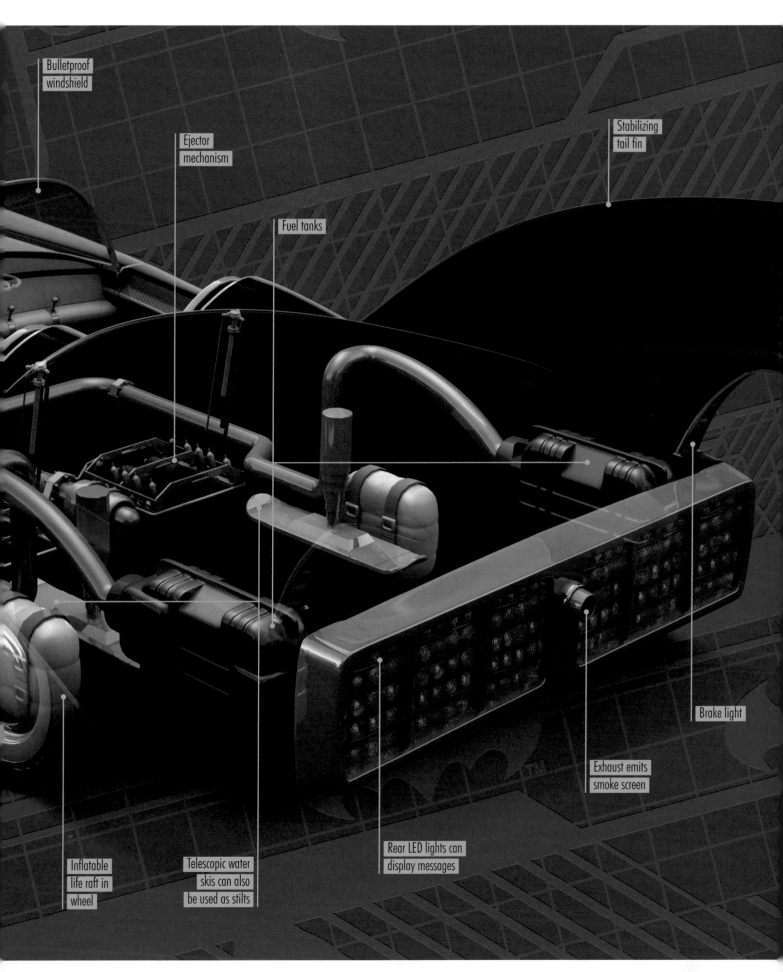

Bulletproof
windshield

Ejector
mechanism

Stabilizing
tail fin

Fuel tanks

Brake light

Exhaust emits
smoke screen

Rear LED lights can
display messages

Inflatable
life raft in
wheel

Telescopic water
skis can also
be used as stilts

EDITOR

Richard Jackson

WRITERS

Alan Cowsill

James Hill

Richard Jackson

VOLUME EDITOR

Jo Bourne

TECHNICAL CONSULTANT

Stephen Norton

GENERAL EDITOR

Ben Robinson

PROJECT MANAGER

Jo Bourne

ILLUSTRATORS

Ed Giddings

Adam 'Mojo' Lebowitz

Alex Pang

Roger Stewart

COVER DESIGNERS

Terry Sambridge

Steve Scanlan

DESIGNERS

Terry Sambridge

Katy Everett

PACKAGING DESIGNER

James King

With thanks to:

Neil Corry

R Guy Sawtell

Copyright © 2018 DC Comics.
BATMAN and all related characters and elements
© & ™ DC Comics.
WB SHIELD: ™ & © Warner Bros. Entertainment Inc. (s18)

EAGL41213

Batman created by Bob Kane and Bill Finger

Illustrations originally published in BATMAN ™ AUTOMOBILIA,
by Eaglemoss Ltd. 2018